About the Author

E.A. Blare has always loved to write, but throughout childhood, his ambition was to travel the world. His first chance came after school when he got a scholarship to America where he studied, and partied, for a year! He then decided to explore the world further and travelled around America, Australia and the West Indies, working in a variety of jobs including milkman, telephone engineer, bank clerk, postman and jack-hammer operator!

When his wanderlust was satisfied, E.A. Blare got married and settled down in a gritty part of London. The settings and characters in *Wising Up* are drawn from his experience of bringing up four children in this environment. He now lives in Berkshire and writes full-time.

D1386156

For Lindy and Dad

wising up

wising up

e.a. blare

 ORCHARD BOOKS

ORCHARD BOOKS
96 Leonard Street, London EC2A 4XD
Orchard Books Australia
14 Mars Road, Lane Cove, NSW 2066
First published in Great Britain in 2000
A paperback original
Text © E.A. Blare 2000
The rights of E.A. Blare to be identified as the
author of this work have been asserted by him
in accordance with the Copyright,
Designs and Patents Act, 1988.
A CIP catalogue record for this book is
available from the British Library.
ISBN 1 84121 557 0
1 3 5 7 9 10 8 6 4 2
Printed in Great Britain

contents

part one

As he walked away from her door Ritch wished he could go back and start over again.

Knowing what I do now, he thought, everything would turn out OK. I wouldn't go crazy that night in the heatwave. And I wouldn't make Ice look such a fool during the break-in. I'd listen to G. I'd listen to Alex. But life isn't like that. You only go around once…

At first it was just the same old routine. Ritch's mum and her boyfriend had gone down the pub. He'd stayed in bed all day reading that week's *Shoot!* magazine. It was the third time he'd read it.

Although he lived in the south Ritch supported Manchester United. They played football for purists – skilful, all-out attacking stuff. You never heard of them being held to a dull nil–nil draw.

Eventually, without any plans about what was going to happen, he'd left the flat. The kid needed some air. Getting stuck on a girl was the last thing on his mind.

Both lifts were broken so Ritch used the stairs. Halfway down he heard the drugs school scatter and, passing that landing, breathed in the fumes.

Cleaning fluid or some other muck.

The stink made him feel sick. He hated junkies. Rocks, needles or solvent, he thought, it's all the same poison. A kid in the next block had died sniffing petrol last year.

His best buddy, G, lived on the quiet side of the estate and he took the shortcut through the alley that ran by the flats.

Round at the garages Sharon Blake was hanging out with a girlfriend and a couple of guys.

'Hiya, Ritch.'

She tossed her head.

'OK, Sharon?'

Her hair looked good, she'd let it grow...but they were history.

'Why don't you come over later? I'm babysitting,' she offered.

'Maybe some other time.'

Ritch carried on walking.

On the far side of the kids' playground he climbed the sheds and then dropped into the street.

Across the road the houses were older but much better kept. Aspen Village. It used to be a flash address once. It was still full of snobs who had solid careers. Bank managers, stiffnecks like that.

They must have been gutted when the estate got built. Every one of them would give their right arm to move out, but they had no chance. Nobody was going to buy a house next to that dump unless the price was a give-away. So they had to put up with it. Ritch guessed they were stuck too. Like him. His heart really bled.

G's family rented a flat above an off-licence on the estate side of the road. There were two under-age kids outside looking for a front man to score them some booze.

'Going to a party, fellas?' Ritch said. They weren't bad kids.

He held out his hand. The coins were hot from where the shorter one had been holding them.

'Thanks, Ritch. You're a pal.'

They'd probably been waiting there ages. He went in and bought them a fourpack, keeping the loose change and one of the beers.

He always got served easy. Pubs were no problem, either, except for the local where his old lady drank. Ritch was on the tall side, medium built, and he'd been shaving since he turned fourteen almost two years before. Most days he had a thick stubble. His old man looked sort of Italian and everyone said that Ritch favoured him.

The kids disappeared fast. They'd copped a good deal. He could have ripped off their money and left them with nothing.

Ritch popped his beer open and the off-licence manager stared at him through the window. The guy yawned, a jaw-breaker. He'd seen the whole deal. As long as things looked OK on the security camera inside the shop he wasn't bothered. The peanuts they paid him, why should he care?

Ritch downed the beer and lobbed the empty over a wall before hanging on G's doorbell. His folks weren't too crazy about them being best pals.

'Yes?'

It was the old man, looking right through him.

'Is G there?' Ritch asked. For crying out loud, the guy knew who he was all right. His son and Ritch had been buddies for years.

'Geoffrey's studying.'

'I'll wait for him.'

The guy shut the door in his face and left him standing there. Ritch was used to it. Once, he used to think that G's people didn't like him because he was white. Then G put him straight. They wanted their son to get on, they thought Ritch was a bad influence. For some reason he didn't feel quite so bad after that.

Finally G put in an appearance.

'I wish he wouldn't do that,' he said, scowling over his shoulder. He was stick thin and wore glasses but could act pretty ticked when he wanted to, which was most of the time.

'He never said you was out here,' he went on. 'Lucy told me.' His little sister.

'No sweat,' Ritch said. 'Did you get it sorted?'

He was still suspended but G had real prospects. The poor kid's family planned on him going to college. They wanted him to study Law – from the right side.

G shrugged. 'Most of it.'

'So what's new, hotshot?'

'Nothing. Same old bull. We've got mocks all next week.'

Ritch wouldn't keep him out late. He couldn't

hack the academic trip, not since a long way back. He wasn't about to screw up G's chances though.

They decided to go down the Mission, which was no big surprise – that was the only free action in town. Apart from the small change Ritch had made off those under-age drinkers they were flat broke. G's family had hit on hard times. On Saturdays Ritch helped out at the market, cash in hand. But this was Friday and he knew better than to ask his mum for a loan.

Mission, that's what everyone called the place. Ritch couldn't remember the real name if he ever knew it. It was this 'youth' hangout near the flats. The Church ran it like they were missionaries out in the bush.

Ritch spent the loose change on a bag of prawn crackers from the Blue Orchid take-away. G grabbed a handful and they walked along eating. Neither of them said very much. Both were too deep in their own thoughts. You don't always need to be talking if you're close mates.

When they'd almost got there Ritch asked G, had he thought about death lately? What would be the worst way of dying?

'Watching all those video splatterflicks is having a

morbid effect on you.' G shook his head and took some more crackers. 'You ought to read a good book for a change.'

Ritch laughed out loud. Around that neighbour-hood kids who read books, not porn or betting slips, were rarer than unbroken car windows. G was the only one that he knew.

At the next corner, where they made their turn, some moron was wrecking a pay-phone. It wasn't even the type with a cash-box. It only took phonecards. What a sad waste of effort. What a dumb waste of time.The Mission lights came in sight and all at once Ritch didn't feel up for it. He still couldn't shake the thought of those junkies out of his brain: huddled up on the stairs, slowly killing them-selves...

'I reckon I could take anything except drown-ing,' he said. 'That's the one thing that would freak me.'

When Ritch had first started school the old man had taken him and his brother eel-fishing down by the canal. Trying to tightrope across the bridge handrail, he'd fallen in.

The water was more like scum soup. He swallowed

it, choked on it, breathed it and sank. They pulled him out fast but not fast enough for Ritch. For years after he gave the place a wide berth. Sometimes he still had bad dreams.

He balled up the cracker bag and volleyed it at a car passing by, a current-reg. Porsche running through to the motorway. G stooped to pick a chunk of glass out of his trainer. He gave his buddy the look you reserve for crazies down at the bus depot.

Ritch wiped his hands on his jeans. G straightened up and said, 'I guess we've all got a breaking point. Come on, you'll feel better once you've knocked some mug off the pool table here.'

When they got there Father Thomas was sitting in his office by the main entrance.

'Good evening, Ritch. Good evening, Geoff,' he said, then shook their hands. 'We haven't seen you in a while. Where have you been hiding?'

He was a decent enough old geezer, the best of the bunch. Ritch always wondered when he'd last dragged a comb through his hair. He had this big, wild, white mess of it.

'We've been around, Father,' he answered. 'Here and there. How's the-pie-in-the-sky business doing?'

'Why? Are you thinking of turning over a new leaf?'

Ritch laughed. 'You know me. Live hard now, 'cos when you're dead you're done.'

The old guy's lips pursed but he took it all right. He'd never been one to preach at you. Not like the others.

'Well now, Ritch, we'll have to agree to disagree on that one.' He waved them through. 'Otherwise I might find myself out of a job.'

'You'll have plenty of company if you do, Father,' said G. His old man, a baker, had just got laid off.

The pair strolled on into the poolroom. Kenny and Muff were playing the table. They'd left school last summer and still hadn't found work yet. You could say that looking at them was like seeing your future right now.

Ritch said, 'Hi,' chalked up his name for a game and checked out the play while G shot the breeze with some kid he knew.

Right away Ritch saw that Kenny was onto a hiding. He'd gone three balls behind and Muff had three pockets covered. The whitewash was just a few shots away. Bored, Ritch took in the room. There were the usual punters, male and female. Most of these sad cases never went anyplace else. Then he spotted a couple of new faces. Girls. One plain. One foxy.

They'd dressed down for the occasion but their jewellery looked too expensive, and their shoes. That, plus their 'casual' rubbernecking the natives, gave them away. They stood out like dots on a domino.

'Oi, Ritch. You're on.' Muff rubbed off the two names above his on the blackboard. 'These guys said they want to scratch.'

Kenny patted his shoulder and passed him the cue.

'Go get him.' He grinned. 'Kill him. He slaughtered me.'

Kenny didn't really mind losing to Muff, they were a team. You never saw either out solo for long.

Muff broke and then started knocking them in. He was onto a hot streak. Ritch chalked his cue and inspected the new girls. The foxy one, a long-haired brunette, had a cool way about her. Very cool...full of class.

Muff's killer streak died on him. It was Ritch's turn to perform. Sussing angles, he moved round the table. The brunette slipped out of the way and smiled. So she wasn't stuck up, the class was genuine enough.

On his night Ritch wasn't a bad player. This happened to be one of those times. He had the rub of the green here and there and he beat Muff in one visit. The little guy whinged some but that's how the breaks went. G had called it right on the money. Ritch felt more upbeat for sure.

Next he took on Big Tony. On Saturdays, down at the market, Tone heaved sacks of spuds around like they were packets of crisps, but he couldn't shoot pool any day. Ritch was hitting his stride when in waltzed Ice, mobhanded as always. The skinhead belched and shoved the plain girl out of his way.

Sticking out his chin the bald thug displayed a brand-new tattoo – CUT HERE – on his throat. All round, the temperature dropped. Someone stood up and walked out. One of Ice's boys went up to the board and erased all the names. Bad news.

If players wanted to scratch that was their business. You didn't do it without their saying so. But no one argued. So, hey, Ritch finished Tone off and asked, 'Who's next?' like nothing had happened. He wasn't into fighting other kids' battles unless it was G.

'Who's next?' Ice mimicked and spat on the floor. 'What's up – you blind? Or just stupid?'

All his boys laughed way too loud. A real bunch of crawlers.

'Rack 'em and break.' Ritch leaned on his cue, half smiling. 'Talk's cheap, ain't it.' He hated the creep.

The softer kids eased out the door. G came round his side of the table and out the corner of his eye Ritch saw the plain sort wanting to go, but the brunette refuse.

Ice chalked and broke without sinking anything. He wasn't happy. A stunted pit bull with low self-esteem, he sneered, 'Win or lose, you're on your bike, son,' and picked his swollen tattoo.

Nice and easy, not rushing, Ritch made a string of shots, setting himself up and nudging Ice where he wanted him. By the time he stepped back he had one ball left, teetering over a pocket, and Ice had nothing to go for with a nasty bridge to make too.

Stretching across the cloth, Ice planted his nicotined fingers and fouled the cue ball. Instead of getting up he went ahead with his shot. Ritch reached out and snatched the white as it screwed down the table.

'Game over, Ice,' he said, tossing the ball in the air and then catching it. 'First rule of the table, cheats get thrown off.'

He thought, who's laughing now?

'You what?' Ice came towards him, sliding one hand inside his windcheater. The strip lighting above flashed on his greasy shaved head.

'Say that again.' He kept on coming.

Tone, Kenny and Muff ghosted in behind Ritch, pushing G out of the way. Ritch motioned them back. This was his beef. Ice, the gutless creep, pulled out an evil-looking blade. It had a serrated edge on one side like some kind of carving knife. Everyone rushed to get out of the room but Ice's crew had blocked off the exit. A girl screamed.

Ritch let him get closer, not too close, then he drew back his arm. Ice pulled up sharp. His face started to sweat.

Ritch could see the creep wondering would he

cop the cue ball between the eyes or get through with his blade first?

'Your move, hard man,' he said, pushing it. If he missed he still had the pool stick in his other hand.

Ice licked his lips. He glanced round the room. The rat needed a way out. He couldn't back down in front of that crowd.

'You'll get yours, don't worry,' he promised.

Suddenly the yob turned and stumbled out, slicing a gash the length of the table. Which more or less put an end to the night's entertainment. And that was how that thing between Ice and Ritch got started. No big deal. But in the end it changed Ritch's life. No way for the better. And in the long run for good.

The room emptied in a rush like a river bursting a dam.

Ritch felt brassed off over the table. It'd had a nice feel to it. Even if they did a good job of re-covering it, it wouldn't play the same.

Most of the kids decided to slip out the back way before the damage got discovered. Tone, Kenny and Muff split together in case Ice was still lurking around. Since there was nothing to stay for, Ritch headed back towards G's place. It was shaping up to be an earlier night than he'd figured on.

Outside, G said, 'You're crazy, you know that?' his voice shaking. The kid was really upset. 'Don't you ever think about consequences? From now on you're gonna have to watch your back. All day. Every day.'

He didn't like any kind of trouble, let alone knives. Over the years Ritch'd had to bale him out of plenty of tight spots. That's how they'd got to be buddies. G was a pacifist so Ritch kept an eye on him. Yet somehow G still argued that his way was best.

Ritch said, 'Don't worry, I've got that little runt's number. If he wants any more I can take care of him.' No one pushed him around without him pushing back twice as hard. Out of pride.

Not that he claimed to be the meanest kid on the estate. He left that to Ice and his crew. The jerks liked to think they had a reputation to live up to. To Ritch, the whole gang were a joke. On their own they were nothing. And like G always said, in a bunch their total brains wouldn't add up to a fool's.

Up ahead Ritch saw the two new faces from the Mission hurrying past a boarded-up shop-front and then the Chinese. They were rattling along at a fast pace. The plain one clung tight to the foxy one's arm, keeping her eyes on the ground. Could be they were lost.

The brunette held her head high in the air. She was something to see. It would take more than a rough neighbourhood to faze her. She'd stay cool in an earthquake. Her buddy didn't look too bad, G was game, so they caught them up.

'Did you have fun? Or were you disappointed?' Ritch asked, coming alongside.

Her friend jumped but she just said, 'How is that any business of yours?'

He had to laugh, she acted so tough.

The girls carried on walking and the lads fell in step. Talking across Ritch, G asked her friend where they came from. She told him Aspen Village. What a surprise. G said he lived over the off-licence. Were they going that route? He spoke to her as if she was his sister. She quit memorising the pavement and looked at him, interested. In a frail kind of way he was a good-looking kid.

While they were jawing Ritch sized up the brunette. She had green eyes and a wide mouth. She didn't wear any make-up, there was no need.

G's chat petered out so Ritch said, 'Were you slumming or visiting?'

Most times that stuff annoyed the hell out of him.

Her buddy said, 'For a dare.'

At the same time she said, 'Slumming, of course.'

He laughed harder and in spite of herself the brunette let a smile show. Which didn't stop him winding her up even more.

'So you think you're better than us?'

G winced. He needn't have worried, nothing dented her cool.

'I can't say that I'm a great admirer of violence.' She had an accent, a bit plummy. Not grating though.

'Sometimes you've got to fight fire with fire,' Ritch countered.

'Arsonists start fires because they enjoy the flames.'

She rammed his cliché into the ground.

By then the other girl and G had dropped behind. She must have felt safe with him because she'd taken his arm. Ritch wasn't doing so good. This brunette was hard to impress, and razor sharp. He asked her name.

'Alex. And yours?'

'Ritch.'

'Short for Richard?'

'No, just Ritch. With a t.'

He couldn't keep his eyes off her. She had slender fingers and narrow nails. Plus a nice, relaxed, swinging walk. On impulse he tried to take her hand but she saw him coming a mile away.

Quickly folding her arms she said, 'Am I supposed to find you irresistible or something?' Close enough: he could double for the singer in her favourite band.

'Most girls have up to now.'

He was no pretty boy but he did OK.

Super cool, she made a sound in her throat as if she was clearing it.

'Perhaps they didn't notice your flaws. Your teeth, for instance.'

'They did. But it never bothered them. Nor me.'

Dentists had never been his favourite people. He opened his mouth to show her the stumps. She peered inside.

'My brother did it,' he explained. 'The week he went in the army.'

They'd thrown a few punches while watching boxing on TV. Sparring around, it spiralled out of control. You know the kind of fun. One accidental knockout leads to another.

Billy was a nice enough guy. He'd looked out for the old lady and Ritch, after the old man did a runner, till she found her feet. Then once her first boyfriend moved in he ducked out of the picture. Ritch couldn't say that he blamed his big brother. Although it sounded like his idea of a nightmare, from Billy's letters he was happy being a squaddy. There was no accounting for taste.

Alex was staring at him as if she thought he'd taken offence.

'It was sort of an unintentional going-away present,' Ritch told her. 'I kinda like it.'

The relieved expression on her face lasted all of two seconds. She didn't want to seem over-keen.

'You mean that you think that it makes you look rugged,' she claimed.

'I don't "look". I'm the real thing.'

She let out her breath in a loud hiss. 'You're not

exactly modesty personified, are you?' Despite that, he was just the sullen kind of boy she adored. And her parents would hate.

'Personi-what?'

He didn't get what she meant but she didn't look down her nose at him. Given a chance, kids from the Village tried to come it. She didn't. She spoke her mind, that's all. She always did.

Ritch glanced back down the street. G and his girl were going great guns. He was whispering in her ear and she kept tittering.

Alex looked too. 'Hurry up, Clare,' she called out and cracked on the pace. 'Would you really have thrown that ball at him?' she asked.

'Right in his ugly face,' Ritch admitted. Just like her, he believed in telling it straight. They were close enough for him to feel her recoil.

'How awful.'

'It was him or me.'

'People shouldn't be that way.'

'They are where I come from.' A dog-eat-dog world.

He'd brought them to the road that separated the estate from the Village. They stopped. It was like coming to a frontier. Neither of them knew what to say.

'I'll bet everything's not perfect over there,' Ritch said at last, not too roughly. 'Hasn't your old man ever been burgled?'

She caught his drift. 'Yes we have.' Her eyes flashed red hot. 'But my father would never hurt anyone. Not over a VCR or a stereo, never mind your stupid pool match.'

Somewhere he'd hit a raw nerve. He dropped the subject. They stood waiting for the others. Alex: she was genuine, feisty, smart as a whip and a looker. Some combination. And all the while only this road lay between.

Maybe I ought to walk home with you,' he suggested. 'You wouldn't want to bump into anything nasty.' He meant what he said. He hated to think of her running into some junkie mugger.

She was still angry at him.

'Isn't that a little like the kettle calling the pot black?' Then she picked herself up. 'Oh, I'm sorry.'

'What for?' He wasn't uptight. He never claimed to be any angel.

Her head half turned. 'I didn't mean anything.' She was blushing.

G and Clare came along, arm in arm.

Ritch got the picture.

'No sweat. I know you didn't. That PC stuff don't exist round our way, does it, G?'

'No. Everyone's too mentally challenged.'

His 'date' laughed. She was all over him.

'Shall I walk home with you, then?' Ritch asked Alex again. Clare gave her an encouraging smile and G grinned.

She kept them wondering. But not for too long. Finally she said to Clare, 'We'll probably get stopped by the police.' In pairs they all crossed the road.

Alex asked what school Ritch went to and he said he didn't, not lately. Being told what to do and how to think wasn't his idea of high jinks. She frowned and told him that she was in the sixth form at an all-girls' miles away. Clare, her cousin, went there too. They lived near each other and were both into indie bands. Ritch told her about his head-banger brother and she said he should count himself lucky. She didn't have any brothers or sisters at all.

Too quickly they arrived. Tasty motors lined the street – Jags, Mercs, BMWs – all well alarmed. Even so they'd make any half-decent car booster drool.

Alex stalled Ritch at the gate of a fake-Tudor semi while Clare and G dawdled past. The place came with its own garage and a front lawn mowed in stripes like Wembley's Cup Final pitch. Footsteps faded as the other two rounded the corner, then everything went quiet.

Alex smiled. Boy, what a smile. Softly she said, 'Goodnight, Ritch,' and put out her hand. She'd learned the hard way to keep her family and boyfriends apart. He stuck his in his pockets. 'Don't I get to walk you to your door?'

'Nothing's likely to happen to me between here and there.'

'You never know,' said Ritch.

'Oh, yes I do.' If she kept this hunk eager he might come back one day.

'You can't be too careful.'

'Precisely – I agree.'

A rentacop security van cruised down the street and in a house nearby someone switched on the radio. Opera blared out then fell to a murmur. Alex dropped her hand to the gate and felt for the latch.

'Don't I get a kiss?' Ritch sounded desperate.

'I don't even know you.' Her hip touched his.

'Well there's no time like the present. Let's make a start.'

She opened the gate but didn't go in. The pathway was gravelled just like their drive.

'Our neighbours don't miss a thing,' she said, 'and my parents...'

'If a kiss on the doorstep's all they have to worry about they must be doing all right,' he complained.

No pay parties. No bailiffs. No reeking lifts.

Up at the house the porch light came on. From somewhere inside a man's voice called out, 'Alex? Is that you?'

These days her parents crowded so close that she couldn't breathe.

'Listen, Ritch, you'll have to go or they'll nag.' She pulled a face like, What a bore. 'Thanks for walking me here. It was very considerate and I enjoyed having our chat.'

At that moment the curtains cracked at an upstairs window, most likely a bedroom. A woman's face appeared, covered in cream, scowling down at the pair. Alex waved hello. The dragon banged on the window.

The curtains closed and the shadow moved away. A door slammed.

'I must go. Really.'

She wanted to stay. He looked so disappointed. Such a glowering face.

As an arc of light flooded out of the front door, or maybe before, he didn't know, Ritch kissed her cheek. She darted through the gate and tore up the path.

'Goodnight,' they both called out at the same time.

That gravel made a heck of a racket. Ritch guessed Alex's people didn't think a burglar would have the smarts to stick to the grass. He wandered to the end of the street and hung around waiting for G, admiring the cars. Here we go again, he thought. He'd never been flavour of the month with anyone's parents. Even his own old lady could have too much of him.

*

There was nothing going on anywhere. The whole place was dead. Ritch and G mooched round the estate for an hour then called it a night. Ritch's old lady and her boyfriend were in when he got home. They'd ducked back to change, collect her beat-up Escort and skip on to a nightspot.

His mum hurried out of the bathroom and nearly ran over him.

'Hello, handsome.' She pinched his cheek and took a pull on her cigarette. She always had one fired up. 'What have you been up to?' Without waiting for an answer she swept off down the hall, to their room.

Ritch shut the door and said, 'I nicked a Ferrari. It's waiting outside,' but she didn't hear.

The TV in the front room was churning out some crummy quiz. Ritch switched it off and heard the same crud booming next door. So he found his favourite wildlife show on Terrestrial and racked out on the couch.

Gerry the Jerk slithered in.

'How's it going, mate?' He stood in front of the set while he did up his tie.

The guy stunk of booze. Ritch moved his head to watch a game warden in India who was searching for poachers. They were hunting tigers to extinction, just for their bones. Gerry took the hint and slithered back to the bedroom.

The sap hadn't got totally wrecked yet. But he was well on the way. They both were. And there was no point saying his old lady should use a cab, she'd only claim that the club was just down the road.

Ritch wished she would listen when he warned her about driving boozed. Or about Gerry being a free-loading creep, taking her for every penny she owned. He was ten years younger than her. Since picking up with him she'd dressed way too showy. Ritch guessed that it must have been something to do with her age, she was forty last year.

His old lady lurched in with the sponger in tow. She was tall, just like Ritch, only a blonde. The Jerk was a lot shorter though he always wore stack-heeled boots – as if that would fool anyone.

'Is it this Monday or next that I've got to see your headmaster?' she asked, biting down on her cigarette and fastening her leopardskin coat.

'I dunno. Does it matter?' The ads had come on. Ritch fished out the remote from under a cushion and began channel-surfing.

'Vera, down the Cowshed, said she'd do my hair.' She unplugged the cancer stick, aiming a kiss at his ear. 'There's a TV dinner next to the microwave. Be a good boy now.'

As if he had any choice.

'We won't be long,' she promised.

Gerry moved out of her shadow like a snake coming out from a rock.

'He'll be OK.' He put on his all-boys-together voice. 'He's probably got some little bird dropping by. Ain't you, mate?'

The guy was so oily he made Ritch want to puke. He remoted the volume right up. Stuff the neighbours. Their three-day parties were famous. It was their turn.

His old lady blew him a kiss, said, 'Bye, sweetheart,' and rushed out the door. Wherever they were off to they were probably late.

Ritch thought, no way is he good for her.

Mind you, none of them had been. She could be a fair judge of some people. When it came to the men in her life, forget it, she didn't have a clue.

Take her and the old man, the mismatch of the century. She followed all the soaps and he watched subtitled movies. She read the tabloids while he took a broadsheet. She loved a knees-up. He liked a night in with a book. Why did they marry? Ritch couldn't figure it. Whatever pleased one was bound to make the other one miserable. And that made them bitter, as if it was some deadly insult. In the end you never saw them happy together. They fought all the time. One day he packed his suitcase and they never saw him again. What a nice guy.

Ritch's stomach started to rumble. Since breakfast he'd only had those prawn crackers. He left the TV blasting away. The kitchen was a tip and the dinner turned out to be liver and onions. There was nothing better to nuke so he grabbed a pork pie from the fridge.

His room had bad breath. Ritch threw the sheets in the wash and sprawled on the mattress. Picking up where he'd left off, he read his copy of *Shoot!* and then started over again. There was an article about injuries that had finished players' careers, with some horrible photos that made his flesh crawl.

For a while Ritch lay staring up at Billy's bare top

bunk. On Monday he and his old lady were supposed to go up the school. But he wasn't going. He'd talk her out of it, no worries. He was never going back. In a few months he'd be sixteen. What could they do to him then?

Besides, they were as sick of Ritch and his games as he was of theirs. The first two years hadn't been too bad. After that it was hassles all the way. He'd nearly got expelled once for hot-wiring his head-of-year's Metro then dumping it in a 'red' bus lane. Add some fights and the truanting and his whole school history was there.

Ritch had copped his latest suspension for telling the fool who was supposed to coach them at football that he couldn't trap a bag of cement in the wet. As deputy headmasters go, the guy was a dunce. Rules, discipline, punishment – it was all a big bunch of bull anyhow. Just a way for them to control you...

A thought struck him. He bet Alex's parents paid for her to go to that school and she had to wear a uniform with a blazer, a tie, and some lousy hat. Poor kid. He bet they made her life hell.

Ritch fell asleep dreaming about England's prospects for the coming World Cup. His old lady and her boyfriend fell through the door at three in the morning. The noise woke him up. He found a blanket and crawled under it. He had to be up at seven the next day to earn some cash down on Big Tony's market stall.

He saw Alex again that Sunday.

Across the estate everyone was sleeping off their lunchtime drink down the boozer or half-watching TV. Gerry snored on the sofa while Ritch's old lady sat glued to an omnibus soap. When the walls began to close in on him Ritch took a walk. Maybe he'd run into Ice...

Mick's mini-cab joint had bought a new poker machine.

'Where to, Ritch?' Mick joked as usual.

The drivers loafed around in the back complaining about the lack of fares and goofing off. He gambled some silver away, gave the machine a whack and said, 'If that thing ever pays out I'll take a ride to Land's End and back.'

He drifted over to G's to see whether he'd come back from watching his kid brother play basketball. G

had, but needed to spend the afternoon studying...
Since it was only over the road Ritch took a stroll
through the Village. He figured, why not? There was
nothing better to do.

Pretty soon he came to Alex's house. The garage
doors were ajar and their car was gone. Probably out
for a ride in the country. Ritch hated all that happy
families garbage. He couldn't wait to get a place of
his own.

A black cat slunk out of the bushes and moaned
at the front door. Cats ain't stupid, he thought. Sure
enough the door opened and Alex appeared. The
cat leapt into her arms, she petted it. She was only
wearing a sweatshirt and cut-offs but from where
Ritch was standing that shape would have looked
fine in rags.

He stopped at the gate. She saw him and
checked out the street before nodding agreement.
He lifted the latch quietly and walked on the grass.

'Hello, Ritch.' She brushed the hair out of her eyes.
'What are you doing over this way?' As if she didn't
know.

He stroked the cat. Alex was tickling its chin. It
purred like a machine-gun.

'Don't worry,' he said. 'I don't break and enter on Sunday. It's my day off.'

She smiled a little and leaned her hip on the door frame.

'That's just as well.' Her eyes scanned the house opposite. 'The whole street's asleep but they're still all at home. Except for my parents. They went to my grandmother's for lunch.'

'Why didn't you?'

'Homework.' She made a sour face and the cat arched its back.

'Your friend Geoff seems to have lost interest in my cousin,' she accused. 'He promised to call her on Saturday. Perhaps he forgot.'

Meaning he'd blown Clare out.

'That's G.' The guy was a regular Romeo. What could he say? 'Ain't your feet cold?' She hadn't bothered with shoes.

She didn't answer. Along the street someone put out the milk bottles. Alex started to say something and then changed her mind. The cat mewed like he had a pain.

'What's up with him?' Ritch asked her.

'It's time for his dinner.'

She gave the house next door a heavy once-over. Although she hated the neighbours she wanted to talk.

'You'd best come in.' She stepped aside. 'You can't stay for long though. My parents are due home at six.' That left plenty of time.

The hall smelled of pine-scented polish. Alex showed him into the lounge and went into the kitchen. Ritch heard her sweet-talking the cat as she opened a can:

'You're hungry, aren't you, darling? Yes, you are.'

Their furniture was antique-looking stuff. Not a piece of chipboard rubbish in sight. At one end a bookcase covered the wall, filled with hardbacks. He took a look. Mainly crime stories and travel. The rest were finance and heavyweight reference books, not one sports magazine.

'Are you all right in there?' Alex called. 'You're awfully quiet.'

'I'm fine,' he answered.

'Would you like coffee or tea?' she called again.

The drinks cabinet looked pretty well stocked.

'Have you got a beer?'

'Father only drinks whisky.'

'That'll do.'

'I don't think so. He'd go crazy. I'll make coffee instead.'

The cabinet was locked anyway.

'Does he mark the bottles?' Ritch hollered.

'It wouldn't surprise me. He loves his single malts to the point of idolatry.'

Ornaments crowded the mantelpiece. It was a real fireplace. Ritch picked up a snuffbox shaped like a pig.

Alex came in. 'Here you go.' She handed him a Greenpeace mug, took the pig and put it right back on its spot. The cat sprang onto the plump leather sofa and burrowed into a crack.

Alex looked at Ritch, then the room, trying to pick out a place for them.

Ritch said, 'Did you get in trouble on Friday?'

'Not at all. I told them that I was going over to Clare's to do homework. And she said that she was coming over to study with me. They'd have kittens if they found out we'd been to that youth club.'

A corny alibi like that, thought Ritch. Her parents must be the gullible type. The whole thing seemed weird. He didn't have to lie to his old lady. She was too wrapped up in her own life to fret about his.

They were still standing.

He said, 'I meant over me.'

'I hope you don't mind.' She grinned. 'I said that you were asking for jumble.'

She held a hand over her mouth, stifling a laugh.

'For the Scouts.'

'And they bought it?'

Alex nodded. Weirder and weirder. The girl must have her reasons. Well, he guessed that at least proved they'd missed the kiss.

'Let's take our coffee upstairs,' she said. 'I never feel comfortable down here.'

'Do they make you pay for the breakages?' Ritch asked and smiled.

She smiled back. 'They're not that bad.' Her parents nagged out of fear and love. It was still hard to take.

On the way up she said, 'Have you been in any more fights?'

'I don't call that a fight.' The cut-offs fitted her perfectly.

She turned and noticed him looking. All she said was, 'That boy who ruined your table looks very vindictive. You ought to take care.'

Now, where had he heard that before?

'I don't go there much,' he told her. He'd never seen eyes that dark shade of green. 'And he's a pussycat. No worries. If he comes anywhere near me I'll hammer the creep.'

Her room was a real mess. Pin-ups of indie bands plastered the walls, the bed hadn't been made and there were clothes scattered everywhere. Ritch felt right at home.

Under the window Alex had set up a study desk. On it, beside a computer, an angle lamp shone on some textbooks and an open note-pad. She had a portable TV on the floor, between the desk and the bed, and a nice CD player. Across her bookshelf he saw plenty of hardbacks, just like downstairs.

Alex sat on the edge of the bed while Ritch spun around in her swivel chair.

'What're you studying?' he asked her as he swung past.

'*The Tempest.* Have you read it?'

'What's that?'

'Shakespeare. A play.'

He laughed. 'Are you kidding?'

'It's for my English A-level.'

He gave the spinning a rest. 'I ain't interested in passing exams.'

'What about your future?' She sipped her coffee and looked at him as if he were an alien. One she fancied like mad.

'What future?'

'Very nihilistic, I'm sure.' She tutted. 'You'll regret it one day.'

'You sound like my old gran.' It was a manner of speaking. All his grandparents were dead.

'She must be a very nice person then.'

He didn't have the heart to correct her.

She blew into her mug. 'Seriously, don't you want to be able to get a career and take care of your parents when they get old?'

How could she ask that with two minders like hers? Ritch stuck his coffee on the table and toyed with the computer.

'My old lady won't last that long. She smokes like a chimney.'

'You shouldn't say that.'

She wrinkled her nose and the freckles on it bunched.

'Why not? It's true. Anyhow, you need experience to get a job. And you need a job to get experience.' He was going to say, it's easy for you.

'Not that old saw.'

Alex leaned across, put her coffee next to his and tapped at the keypad. The screen blanked. This boy needed help.

She said, 'That's only an excuse for not trying. What's wrong? Are you afraid you might fail?'

A lock of her hair fell over one eye. Ritch tucked it back in the clip.

'You think I lack confidence?'

'In some ways, yes. In others, no.'

He slid onto the bed and they kissed long and hard. She screwed up her eyes and kept her lips closed. Still, it was some clinch. Boy, he thought, you never can tell. Yet when he tried to touch her she acted as if it was a big shock. She pulled away so fast his lips hung in midair.

'No, you mustn't.' Red-faced with anger she stood up and rifled through the CD stack.

He thought, you idiot. You've blown it. Now she'll chuck you out.

Alex looked up and said, 'I like you a lot, Ritch—'

He didn't wait for the 'but'. He said, 'How about some hard rock?' and helped her search through the pile.

With the hint of a smile she said, 'Perhaps after this,' and put on an indie band. 'But you shouldn't rush so.'

The full smile was back.

After that they both acted as if they hadn't kissed. The music played. They chatted. Alex said her father was an accountant, her mother taught maths. She wanted to teach too, but English Lit. Ritch said he couldn't understand that – studying for years then winding up back in school.

Alex asked what he wanted to do. Ritch said, nothing much. When he was a kid he fancied being a professional footballer. He'd been good enough to train with the local premiership side, until he turned thirteen and they threw him out because he wasn't putting on weight.

Most people he told that, thought Ritch was shooting a line, but not this girl. She said, 'That's terrible. How could they do something that callous?'

'It happens all the time.' He shrugged. 'Anyhow, now I'll settle for a decent car, someplace to live and being left be.'

That didn't cut it with Alex. She said everyone longed for security, that didn't count as an ambition. So he told her, if he could do anything, he'd be a vet. A vet for wild animals on a game reservation. It was one crazy fantasy he hadn't even told G.

She said, 'You'll have to apply to a college then.'

He laughed and said it was only a dream and that proved it. She heaved a sigh – words failed her – and changed the music to a band Ritch didn't know. Just then a car pulled into the driveway, churning the gravel around.

'Oh no.' She knocked over the CDs in her rush to switch off the player. 'That's my parents' car. They must have left early.' If her family met Ritch they'd ruin it all.

Ritch spied out the window. A Volvo estate, the world's ugliest motor, backed towards the garage like a battleship docking. Alex's old lady slid from the passenger seat and trekked to the front of the house. Her key slotted home in the lock, the snap echoed loud down the hall.

Alex signalled for him to crawl under the bed. Ritch shook his head. The car's left wing grazed the side of the garage. Her old man pulled forward to have another attempt. He wasn't much of a driver. Even in that pig of a motor Ritch could have made it first try, both eyes closed.

Downstairs, her old lady traipsed into the hall. If the old man made it this time they still had a chance. Alex ran to the door and grabbed the handle real tight. Wild-eyed, she clung on.

The car trundled back. Right hand down a bit. Bit more. More.

Footsteps started up the stairs, getting close. Alex opened her mouth to call out. The steps stopped and Ritch heard her old lady making a big fuss of the cat. The Volvo backed into the garage at last. He moved Alex's books, climbed on the desk and pushed the window up, slow.

As he began lowering himself onto the garage she tore herself away from the door.

Ritch whispered, 'See you soon.'

She kissed his forehead. 'Stay out of trouble, Ritch.'

His toes touched and he let go of the sill, falling to a crouch on the tarred roof. Alex shut the window. Flattened against the side of the house, he listened to her old man whistling his way into the hall. The letter-box rattled as the door shut behind him.

Ritch hung over the edge then dropped silently onto the grass. He waited a minute, making sure she was OK, before crossing the lawn and vaulting over the fence.

Along the street he passed a boy racer waxing his pride and joy.

'Great day for it,' Ritch said, dead sociable.

The guy gave him the blank. In that neighbour-hood any stranger posed a big threat. Ritch didn't care. He wondered what kind of food Alex fed to her cat. For his money the puss had earned the run of her fridge.

That Wednesday Billy arrived home on leave. He was stationed abroad at the time. Cyprus, Ritch thought. Anyway, some place in the Med. He checked in at the local B&B then ran round to see his kid brother.

The doorbell chimed in the hall and Ritch lay wondering should he bother to answer it. His old lady was out at her cleaning job. Gerry was meant to be looking for work but he'd probably gone down the betting shop – that was the creep's second home.

The bell didn't stop ringing so Ritch heaved himself out of his pit. It was most likely the milkman, after some cash.

'Yeah. What d'you want?' He kept the security chain on and held back a yawn.

A voice said, 'Jesus, what happened? You sick or something?'

It took Ritch a few seconds to recognise who it was. He could never get used to the military hairstyle. It seemed all wrong on an ex-biker like Billy. Besides, right now the bright light was killing his eyes.

Finally Ritch realised who it was. He said, 'I don't remember you resembling any oil painting first thing in the morning,' and knocked off the chain. 'Come in. You're just in time to cook breakfast...'

Billy peered down the hall.

'Who's about?'

'Relax. Only me.'

Ritch left him to the kitchen and went to put on yesterday's clothes. Some time that week he'd have to go to the launderette. In the corner his dirty washing was festering away.

Billy fixed coffee, cleaned a pan from the sink and began scrambling eggs.

'You know what time it is?' he asked.

He had their old lady's blonde hair and blue eyes but whenever he showed disapproval he looked just like the old man.

'Nope.' Ritch finished dry-brushing his teeth and tasted the coffee. 'Mmm. This is great.'

'Half past twelve.' Billy wasn't going to let his kid brother distract him.

'That early?'

The squaddy threw the empty eggbox at his head, and Ritch stood still and let it connect. His big brother grinned. He wasn't the type to stay brassed off for long.

While Ritch buried the eggs Billy straightened the kitchen. Since joining the army he couldn't stand to see any dirt. Yet when he was biking he used to live for the grease.

'The entryphone's bust.' He folded an old pizza carton and crammed it into the bin. 'I had to get someone on the ground floor to open the door.' That stuff put his back up more nowadays, too.

Ritch said, 'You were lucky the lift just got fixed.'

Billy hauled the rubbish out to the chute, and when he came back Ritch was ready to split. He knew that his brother wouldn't want to hang around for too long.

In the lift Billy said, 'When are you going to get a phone, so I can call you?'

'When my six numbers come up.'

Outside, a gang of small kids were fooling around in the playground, breaking bits off the slide. They recognised Billy and he stopped to give them his change. Only he didn't hand it straight over. He put both fists behind his back and they had to guess which one was loaded. Billy always did that, and they always won. Boy, they loved it. Come to that, so did Ritch.

There was only one pub on the estate and that

was the Drovers. Everyone called it the Cowshed. It wasn't exactly a palace but Billy knew all the regulars. Ritch screwed around shooting pool, winning some, losing some, while his brother sat at the bar, standing drinks, cracking jokes with his mates.

Ritch couldn't understand what the guy saw in the army. But he guessed Billy enjoyed the life, because whenever he felt guilty about moving out he'd try to get the kid to enlist.

Right. Sleeping in barracks with a platoon of squaddies coughing and belching all night. And some brain-dead sergeant to tell you when to get up, how to dress, what to do. When pigs flew. Still, Ritch knew the guy was only thinking of him.

The lunchtime rush died. The afternoon shift at the Cowshed could get pretty gruesome. All those no-hopers slumped in corners, staring out through a pint glass on their way to skid row.

After a while the two brothers caught a bus into town. Billy looked happy. Ritch had to give the man credit, he could bevvy all day without any mood-swings.

They hit a couple of pubs that Billy liked and then took in a curry. It got dark out. In the end they wound up at Kelly's. Although he hardly came home any more the squaddy had kept up his subs.

Kelly's was this nightclub in a basement next to the multiplex. Billy signed in, found a table and ordered their drinks. On-stage the stripper was struggling out of her costume.

Billy called out some friendly advice that made her laugh then said, 'OK, little brother – what's going on?'

Ritch smiled. Shoulder to shoulder they stood the same height. Next year Billy would be an inch shorter than him.

'Not a lot.'

But he told him about meeting Alex the night he whipped Ice at pool. Remembering made him feel sore: it had been a good table. Some day he'd pay the jerk back.

Billy lit up a cigarette. He only smoked when he drank.

'He pulled a blade on you? At the Mission? That little snot?' He exhaled through his nose. 'Someone should break both his wrists.'

'He's nothing. He's got a big mouth, that's all. I can sort him one handed.' Ritch waved his arms in the air. 'Do you mind blowing that in some other direction?'

Not that it would make any difference. The place was well full and everyone seemed to be smoking. There was only one skylight. You could smell the toilets from where they were sitting. Ritch wondered who the owner had bribed to swing the health check his way.

The stripper finished her act and Billy gave her a big hand, although he hadn't been watching. Pity, Ritch thought. She wasn't bad. Out of the blue his brother asked, 'How's the old lady?'

'She's fine,' he said. 'You know, the usual.'

'What's this one like?'

He meant Gerry.

'A regular dynamo. He's supposed to be a plasterer. So far I've only ever seen him get plastered. If the guy had an X-ray they wouldn't find a day's work in him.'

Dressed in her street clothes the stripper came wandering out from backstage. As she passed them, on her way to the bar, she gave Billy a nice smile but he didn't notice. Gritting his teeth he stubbed out his cigarette, mashing it down hard in the tray.

'Yeah,' he said, 'the usual,' then bit his lip.

Ritch felt bad. The poor guy was home on leave for the first time in an age – and he was lousing up the whole evening. But he had to share the load, didn't he? That's what brothers are for.

'Forget about him.' Ritch changed the subject, 'Why the surprise visit?'

Billy explained that he had a wedding to go to on Friday, near Hull. He'd have to leave early next morning to catch the first train.

'They're in kind of a hurry.' He smiled and let one eyelid droop. 'Greener always was careless.'

He told Ritch the guy had once loosed off a green baton round – a plastic bullet – by accident, and it hit his own corporal. That's how he got the nickname. According to Billy, Greener was a walking disaster, the worst ham-fist in the army. And there were plenty of those.

After he finished telling the story Billy took a deep draw on his cigarette. Then he said, 'Tell me more about this Alice of yours.'

'Alex. Her name's Alex.' Personally, Ritch didn't

see the connection between the two subjects. 'She comes from the Village.'

'The Village?'

Billy's eyebrows nearly parted company with the top of his head. Ritch went ahead and filled him in anyway.

'It sounds like you're hot for her,' his brother said.

Ritch shrugged and beckoned the waiter. Billy had 'loaned' him a twenty, it was his turn to shout. The man drank as if he'd had a full pint knocked over once. Ritch wondered how long before they switched to halves. Far away, things were looking blurred at the edge.

He turned back to the table and saw Billy giving him their dad's stare, the full treatment.

'Do me a favour, Ritch,' he said. 'Don't get involved. Not with this girl. There's only one way it can end.'

'What's that supposed to mean?'

Seeing that scowl on his brother's face made Ritch break down and laugh. The waiter arrived and Billy held off till he'd brought back their drinks. Then he piled in.

'Come off it, brother. You know what I'm saying –

don't go getting too serious. A girl like that...she's out of your reach.'

'What are you on about?' The kid laughed again. 'For crying out loud, we've only just met.'

'Remember your kite?'

How could Ritch forget that beautiful monster? She was so big they couldn't get on the bus. They had to cart her the whole mile, all the way to the common.

On a good day, with a strong wind, it was worth while. You could run out of line and still feel her trying to climb higher. But in light winds, forget it. You might sweat for an hour without lifting her off.

Last time they flew her he and Billy were both running flat out, trying to get the crate airborne. A sudden blast hit out of nowhere and she rocketed, bucked, then snagged a tree – right at the top.

Billy cut the line and sighed, 'What a shame.' Ritch said no way, he intended going up after her. They argued. Things got out of hand. Not really a fight. In the end Billy backed down but told his brother to take care.

Halfway up, Ritch realised that Billy wasn't a bad judge. The branches got a lot shorter and thinner.

They bent under his weight. Higher up they grew further apart too. He had to go up on his toes, with one arm round the trunk, and stretch for the next handhold.

He looked down. Billy cupped his hands to his mouth. With the wind blowing the leaves around Ritch couldn't catch what he called. But it wasn't, 'Go on, my son.'

Stretching hard, Ritch reached up. His foot slipped and he dropped faster than a six-axle bulk tanker with a full load.

A clump of branches ten feet below stopped him getting killed. He cracked a rib, that was all. Funny thing, Ritch didn't feel any pain. The adrenalin must have kicked in to numb it.

So he went up and carried her down. Trouble was, by the time he struggled back to the ground all he had left was matchwood.

Ritch still made his brother help him lug the wreckage all the way home. Their old lady hit the roof. Being senior, Billy copped all the flak. Ritch just got dragged up the hospital.

When their old man slogged in from work he agreed the kite was a write-off. He'd have to build them a new one. Their mum put the block on that, quick. The poor sap got slaughtered.

'Give it a rest, pal.' Ritch gulped a mouthful of beer. 'I brought her down, didn't I?'

His brother didn't seem any happier.

'Yeah. And almost got killed in the bargain.'

Another act came on-stage, a comedian in a gold suit and bow tie. Boy, was he going to stink. Which he did, and then some.

'This Alex deal won't wind up going where you want it to,' Billy insisted. 'You're gonna get hurt.' He was refusing to quit.

'Hey, we're talking about a class girl here,' Ritch slapped him down. 'Not some cheap weekend bus ride.'

He heckled the comic. The crowd were already shredding the dope and Ritch didn't hold back. At last Billy gave up and joined in. Sooner or later he had to. Squaddies hate being left out.

Around midnight they rang for a cab. By then Ritch's tank was on 'full'. All he had in his pocket was a fistful of silver. When they got to the flats Billy asked the driver to wait.

'Take care of yourself, you hear?' He gave Ritch a

bear hug. 'And remember my warning.'

'OK, big brother.'

The pavement kept moving around under his feet. Putting his back to the door Ritch punched entry-phone buttons at random. Billy craned up at the flat. A light was on in the old lady's bedroom. They'd had an early night for a change.

He said, 'Tell her I'll call her at work. And don't let him jerk you around.'

'Are you kidding?'

Ritch watched Billy walking away. You wouldn't know he'd taken a drink except for the stiff swing of his arms. Like he was back on parade. He told the cabby to head back to Kelly's... Maybe he'd noticed that stripper's smile after all.

The Volvo rolled down the driveway and pulled into the road. Alex's old man got out and kicked each of the tyres, then he opened the boot to check on the spare.

Lazing behind a tree opposite Ritch thought, I'll bet it's the same thing every Sunday. What a sad geezer. But then he was an accountant, safety first was his game.

Alex's old lady stayed on the porch, poking around in her handbag. Eventually she shut the door, crunched down the path and strapped herself in.

As they went past Ritch got a close squint at them. They were older than you'd expect, more like someone's grandad and granny. Neither of them looked too much like Alex. But then who could?

He crossed the road, imagining their great conversation – how many miles to the gallon, and stuff about school.

Alex raised the window and surveyed the street. She sent him a broad smile. After the first Sunday she was ready for this. Satisfied no neighbours were watching, she dropped some keys.

'It's the one with the tag on.'

Ritch took the stairs two at a time, and burst into the room.

Alex sat in the swivel chair with the cat on her lap. She had her hair pinned up in a twist on the top of her head. But for the jeans she could have been modelling jewels.

Ritch thought, pure class.

He said, 'Thank God for Granny,' and bent down

to kiss her. No heavy number, just like hello.

Instead of returning the kiss she shook her head, and he heard a voice saying, 'Excuse me, please.'

Clare was fidgeting at the foot of the bed, buttoning her raincoat. Without a word she brushed past him and stopped at the head of the stairs. Aiming a stiff smile at Alex she said, 'I'll see you tomorrow.'

Alex handed Ritch the cat along with a look full of scorn. Then she went down to the door to say goodbye to her cousin.

'Are you sure that you won't come along?' Alex's voice drifted in through the window. The sun was edging out from the clouds so she'd left the sash up.

'No, honestly. There are some things I must do.'

Clare sounded ticked. Ritch had a hunch she felt sore over G dumping her. As if he could have stopped that. She should have played harder to get.

He rubbed the tom's ear. 'How was I to know she was here, eh boy?'

But the puss didn't fancy it. And when a cat wants to go he gets out. He flipped onto the bed, bounced off the table and sprang out the window.

Single-handed Ritch had cleared the room in less than a minute. It had to be some kind of record.

He thought, maybe this is going to be one of those days.

'Why so sad?' Alex grinned when she got back. 'Did everyone leave you? Poor thing.'

Going up on her toes she put her hands on his shoulders and planted a kiss on his cheek.

Ritch said, 'Sorry about that.'

'What? Clare, you mean?' Her hair smelled of sandalwood. 'Don't be upset. She can be melodramatic sometimes but it doesn't mean much.'

She let go of his shoulders and picked up her coat.

'We're going out. I'm not having you abseiling from my window again. You might break your neck this time.'

Two feet apart they walked down the street. As they reached each gate she paced a little bit faster.

Outside the last house a woman in a headscarf was weeding a flowerbed. When she glanced up Alex said, 'Hello Mrs Wilson. Do want anything down at the corner shop?' to imply that she was only directing Ritch there. The woman told her no thank you, and looked at him sideways.

At the end of the street Alex said, 'I hate this place. Everyone's so prying and rude.'

Her voice was twisted with anger. For the first time Ritch understood how hard she had to fight for a life of her own.

Where he lived no one fretted over who went with who, unless it involved somebody's husband or a young girl got pregnant. Even then it was no big deal. What was new about that?

To cheer her up he told Alex about Billy, leaving out the stripper at Kelly's. She loved how his brother always made sure the kids got their money. As they left the Village she took his hand and without any discussion they strolled out of town.

'It's sad that he acts that way to your mother.' She squeezed his fingers. 'Don't you think?'

Ritch hadn't gone into details.

'Yeah, maybe. I dunno.'

He didn't want to discuss it.

Along the road a dumb Rottweiler was rolling around in a puddle. Alex put on her coat. The sun had got clouded over. Ritch was only wearing an open-necked T-shirt. He wouldn't care if it snowed.

Right the way out there they talked about every-thing. Death, friendship, religion. They agreed that one friend was all that you needed as long as that friend stayed true. Ritch said he reckoned there was no life after death. Alex hadn't decided. She said all religions sounded equally valid to her.

He said, 'Or phoney,' and she gave him a push.

Alex was so easy to be with. It felt no different from being round G. And whatever you asked her she gave a straight answer. Ritch rated that. He couldn't stand being bulled.

At the common they grabbed a Coke at the snack bar under the windmill, then hiked through the woods.

The lake was deserted, the weather was too chancy for Sunday strollers or picnics. Ritch threw stones at the 'No Fishing' sign out in the middle until Alex made him quit.

'Come here, you.' She thumped the hillock beside her. 'You might hit a duck, then you'd be sorry. Vets aren't supposed to do that kind of thing.'

'I ain't that bad a shot.' He sat down in the grass. 'They were miles away.'

'Throwing stones. Just like an overgrown first year.'

He kissed her. Seriously.

'Still think so?'

All they could hear was the ducks on the water and the faint hum of traffic. For a while they sat without talking and then Alex picked a long blade of grass and tickled his neck.

'You certainly dress like one. Not even a sweater in this changeable weather.'

'Who wants one? I'm hot enough.'

He went to kiss her again but she slipped under his arm.

'A really mature boy wouldn't need to be so aggressive.'

That bust-up with Ice was beginning to haunt him.

Ritch said, 'Give me a break here. The creep tried to cheat. Someone had to slap him down good.'

'Why did it have to be you? And it's not only that.' She twisted the grass stem into a knot. 'Getting thrown out of school—'

'The teachers were jerks.'

'But you want to be a vet, don't you?'

'They just like to shove you around.'

'My, but you're stubborn.'

'Yeah, I know. It's my best feature.'

In a strange way he enjoyed her working him over.

Without any warning he snatched the girl's waist and tickled her, hard.

As soon as he stopped, Alex tore up a handful of grass and tried to ram it down the back of his neck. She had a hot temper, and was pretty strong too.

'Take it easy,' he said. The grass still had some dirt stuck to the roots. 'You'll get muck on my shirt.' He just about fended her off.

'You...you...great ape.'

Angry and laughing at the same time, that was the closest she ever came to using a curse word. Which was something different for Ritch — something he liked.

It started to rain so they called a truce and moved camp through the trees. He piled up some ferns for a seat. Alex took off her coat and they both ducked underneath.

Before long a flash of lightning lit up the sky, turning the woods into a flickering cave. Alex said they'd be much safer out in the open. When the thunder rolled in he told her that the storm was far off yet, no need to move.

The sky lit up again and Ritch counted till the next thunderclap. One. Two. Three…Bang!

'It ain't gonna happen,' he told her. 'It's shifting away.' He didn't want her getting soaked to the skin.

She held his arm and pushed right in against him.

'No, you're wrong. It's heading straight for us.'

The sky darkened. Rain sheeted down. The thunder and lightning crept closer then swept over the spot.

It got hairy. Alex had been right about not staying under the trees. Now there was nowhere to run. Ten million volts zapped all around. But Alex felt safe, she flinched less than Ritch. Smiling at the firework display she gazed into the sky.

After what seemed like an hour the rain slackened off. The air changed. The lightning grew fainter and the thunder died down.

Alex shot Ritch a withering look.

He said, 'I can't be right every time.'

'Once would be an improvement.' She shook the rain off her coat and put it back on.

Just then an old couple wearing matching waxed jackets trudged out of the woods. Gaping hard, as if the youngsters were some kind of peep-show, they rambled close by, forgetting the path.

Loud, so they could hear, Ritch said, 'Some people are just plain dirty-minded,' which worked a treat. The ramblers looked away sharp and the old guy almost tripped.

Alex collapsed in a rare fit of giggles. With the storm gone it felt like they'd just passed a test.

She said, 'For one ghastly second I thought they were my parents,' and let herself fall against Ritch in a heap.

'Why? Do they come here a lot?' he asked, putting an arm round her waist.

'Never. But they both wear Barbour jackets.'

Her folks had him beat. They were professional people – an accountant, a teacher. They were meant to be bright yet they kept Alex on such a tight rein. All *that* would do was make her want to run wild. The pair of dummies. They were professional people all right. Professional fools.

Alex wiped some drops of rain off her chin. Stiff from sitting too long, she pushed him away and knelt up in the ferns. Ritch stood and stretched. The sky still looked dull but the common smelled fresh.

He said, 'What's their problem with boyfriends? That they're strictly for bimbos?'

'Not quite.'

She sighed.

'Not exactly.'

It was like counting the thunder. For a long time she shredded a fern while she worked something out.

'They're mad keen on me going to uni,' Alex said finally. 'That's partly the trouble. Apparently I'm supposed to make them feel proud.'

She tossed the fern in the grass. 'And it has to be Cambridge – where *they* went. Where they met each other.'

Jeez, what a strait-jacket. What kept her in it? Loyalty? Affection? Ritch didn't know.

He prised a rock out of the dirt to try hitting the lake from here, then remembered the ducks.

'Ah, guys are a distraction.' Ritch dropped the rock on some nettles and lounged in the ferns.

'Much worse.' She closed her eyes, thinking back. 'I knew a boy once before we moved here. We went out for quite a long while. I liked him a lot but they chased him away. They said that they didn't want us getting too...intimate.'

She shut up and sat cross-legged, waiting. Although her parents loved Alex they were wrecking her life.

He thought, she probably stayed out past her curfew one night. So what?

'I'm not scared of your family. I'll come round and pick you up any time.' Nothing was going to frighten him off.

Alex's mouth turned up at the corners even when she felt sad. Now, as she smiled – this boy was perfect – it was like winning the lottery, six in a row.

But she said, 'No, wait. I've a better idea. When we do meet again it must be in secret. That way they shan't find out until it's too late.' This time she'd win.

Ritch liked the long-term sound of the plan. 'Does that mean I'll only get to see you on Sundays?'

'It won't be that easy.' She touched his cheek. 'They don't always go out. Some weeks my grandmother has someone else visiting.' She picked some flowers and got busy linking them into a chain. 'Once in a while I can ask Clare to cover me.'

Not that easy? You could say that. About as easy as sneaking gold bullion out of Fort Knox.

Ritch said, 'Do you want me to call you?'

No, he didn't think so.

'Well, you can't ring me. We're not on the phone.'

She draped the daisy chain over his wrist. 'I'll drop a note at your friend Geoffrey's flat. Doesn't he live over the wine shop?'

G's old man would love that.

He said, 'In an envelope? Sealed?'

'Naturally. I'll address it to him but use my red stationery so he'll know it's for you.'

'Sounds foolproof to me.' And Jerk-proof too.

'But no more looking for trouble, Ritch.' Alex shifted closer. 'No more fights.'

Ritch took the chain off his wrist and hung it in her twisted-up hair. She leaned back in the ferns and they kissed. Slowly her lips parted. It was like coming home to a fire after standing too long in the rain.

The sun came out. They walked back to the windmill and she bought them something to eat. A meat pie for Ritch, a prawn bap for Alex. Hot and cold, like the day.

They'd had a great time and after that Ritch *had* to see her. She didn't know it, but he was gone. Totally hooked.

So was she.

part two

Part Two

Eight weeks later Kenny and Muff were up on the sheds watching a hot little Alpha getting pushed through some stunts. It was late afternoon, school had let out, and the show had drawn a big mob of rubbernecks to the car park down by the flats.

Tyres smoking, the Alpha skidded between two jalopies then barrelled right for the sheds. At the last moment the driver yanked on the hand-break and the machine slewed around. It continued spinning, made a full circle and slammed head on into a Passat that had been dumped there, then burnt out, last night.

The mob cheered as the dust settled and the engine cut out. Looking gutted, Ritch clambered out through the sun-roof and spat in the dirt.

Muff reached down to help him shin up to join them.

'Where did you find it?' asked Kenny.

He was a good kid but no mastermind. Unless you hijacked one as it rat-ran through the neighbourhood, there was only one place that side of town where you'd boost an Alpha like that.

'Where do you think?' Ritch grunted. 'Outside the YMCA?'

'You hotdog,' Muff laughed. 'If you were any kind of a driver we could have taken her out for a spin down the coast.'

The crumpled Alpha hissed steam. The rad had blown or the head gasket had gone.

'Nah. She was running on empty,' Ritch said. He was brassed off. You would have believed that the wrecked motor was his.

'That's how it is over there,' Kenny chipped in. 'They're all front, those people. A tasty jamjar outside but no wedge for gassing her up.'

Ritch thought, as if he would know.

A bus ground to a halt at the stop on the street side of the sheds and G leapt off. He threw his school-bag up to his pal.

Ritch caught it and staggered. 'Take it easy,' he groaned. 'You got the whole library here?'

After taking a run-up G heaved himself onto the roof.

'OK, guys?' he grinned all round.

'What kept you?' Ritch swung him his bag back.

'You pushing for head boy or something, G-man?' Muff asked. 'You missed a great crash.'

Ritch put an arm round his buddy. 'Leave the guy

be,' he said. 'Someday he's gonna be a great lawyer.'

G eyed the wrecked motor.

'Thanks. But don't count on me qualifying before they put you away.'

He wasn't joking.

Muff liked him fine, so did Kenny. At times like this, though, they didn't know how to take the guy. Down in the car park the rubbernecks were trashing the Alpha. Kenny and Muff slid off the roof and went to salvage whatever they could.

G pushed his glasses back on his nose. 'I thought you said you wouldn't boost any more cars from the Village?'

Ritch shrugged. 'Some fool left the keys in the ignition.'

It was hard kicking old habits. Borrowing a set of wheels with the keys in somehow didn't count. Besides, if he hadn't crashed he would have taken it back.

'Anyhow,' he changed course, 'how's the search getting on? Have you found one that suits you?'

G had been hunting around for a college.

'That's not so hard,' the scholar replied. 'The

toughest part is getting the grant.'

Ritch believed him.

'You know what they say.'

'What?'

'When making rabbit stew…'

'Yeah?'

'First catch your rabbit.'

He was winding G up. The kid had to sit his GCSEs yet. The work he put in, he was bound to pass them for sure. If not, there was no justice – and in that case why bother studying Law?

G smiled and flicked Ritch a red envelope. 'What sort of luck are you having trying to catch yours?'

Not good, as it happened.

Alex's letter said that she couldn't get out again. Clare had decided to be difficult, it would be one alibi too many, and Alex's grandmother was still down in Eastbourne getting over the flu…

After that day over the common they'd gone out a lot. Alex knew an art movie house way out near her school. They were showing some great re-cut Bogart flicks. Alex hated the gangster stuff so they saw

Casablanca twice, then *The African Queen*.

Ritch took her down to the dog track a couple of times. Both nights they came out ahead. Alex loved it. Then luck ran out on the pair. Her granny had got taken ill and her father was unwilling to drive all that way. Now her cousin was cutting up rough.

'When was the last time you saw her?' G looked away while Ritch re-read the note.

'Last week at the bus stop.'

'I mean on a date.'

'Almost a month ago.'

'It ain't worth the hassle. She's not the only girl in the world. You should tell her it's over. Just say that you quit.'

'No thanks. I don't have your great memory for faces.'

Ritch could never figure out how come his best buddy had so much success with the opposite sex. G changed girlfriends more often than most guys change their socks.

They'd been walking around on the sheds. The roof was covered in old furniture, bike frames and garbage. The two friends scuffed a space clear on the car-park side and sat with their legs hanging over the edge.

Down below, Muff and Kenny had ripped out the car's stereo. Now they were under the hood working on something there.

Up on the second floor a woman looked over the balcony and shouted that she was phoning the Law. Kenny and Muff laughed, 'Go ahead,' and just carried on. G sighed, shaking his head.

Ritch thought, the kid studies too hard.

He said, 'Don't you ever feel like just cutting loose?'

'Are you serious? 'Course I do,' his pal exploded.

'When I'm through with college I'm gonna buy a car and a tent, and drive across Europe to Greece.'

He was always spouting on about Homer and Troy.

'I might go further and see Turkey,' he carried on. 'I want to do something with my life before I get tied down.'

G had never mentioned it till then. *The Iliad* didn't mean anything to Ritch, but the trip sounded great. A car of their own – lots of beaches and fun.

'Why don't I come with you?' he offered.

'What about your sweetheart in the Village?'

'What about your old man?'

Dream on, right? They both laughed, realising it was all just a long shot. But Ritch had a hunch that G was in with a shout.

Kenny and Muff had disconnected the car's battery. They settled for that and let the rubbernecks get back to work.

A guy with shoulders like a bull came out up on the fourth floor and moaned about all the racket. Someone mouthed off at him. He stormed down the stairs.

The mob scattered but Kenny and Muff stood their ground. They were pals of the guy's brother. They sold him the stereo with the battery thrown in for free.

'What is it with those two?' G spat at a beer can below.

'They hustle because they can't find any work.'

It was obvious.

'I don't see them busting a gut looking,' G objected.

'Sure they do. Be fair – some people don't get the breaks.'

'Some people don't even try.'

Ritch guessed that he was comparing them with his old man.

*

There was nothing better to do, so they had a two-aside kickaround against Kenny and Muff, using the can for a ball. When they grew tired of that they fooled around up on the sheds, lobbing stuff at the bus queue.

A row of pensioners' bungalows backed onto the car park. From on top of the sheds you could see into their gardens, right down the row. The side gate of one opened. Ice and a pal slunk inside. The skinhead lashed a boot at a cat on the path. Laughing, they sloped round to the rear and jemmied a sash.

It was Maggie Finn's place. Everyone knew the old girl. She was a widow who ran a shellfish stall on weekends outside the Cowshed. If you were caught strapped for cash, and she liked you, you could eat on the slate.

Muff found a chair and broke off one leg.

He said, 'Let's pulp their kneecaps.' Like a lot of small guys he had his mean side.

G looked worried. 'Why don't we just call the cops then watch the action?' he pleaded.

Supposing they wanted to, there wasn't time. Ice passed a TV set out through the window. Ritch yelled, 'Let's go,' and G included they jumped off the shed roof.

For weeks Ice had been talking big all around the estate. Ritch had better watch out or he was going to cut him up good. It was just so much hot air. The little runt knew where Ritch lived yet had kept out of his way. Now here was the perfect chance to get even. The time had arrived to take him down a few pegs.

Ice had dropped a second pal off outside the gate to cover his back. He'd picked the wrong lookout. One sight of Ritch plus his crew and the wimp ran.

They all eased into the garden and round to the rear. Ice's other buddy was humming to himself with his head stuck inside the window. A toaster lay on the grass beside Maggie's TV. Ritch put his hand over the dope's mouth and hauled him away.

'Keep it buttoned,' he warned. 'And don't stop running, unless you want both your legs broke.'

He threw the sap out on the pavement. Muff aimed a swipe at his butt. Without a peep the kid got up and hared down the road.

Ritch thought, this is gonna taste sweet.

He swung through the window and touched

down in a bathroom. One by one the others followed him. Kenny came last. He knocked a line of shampoo bottles flying. It didn't matter. Somewhere in the bungalow Ice was ripping the whole place apart. He must have believed all the rumours about Maggie hoarding a mint.

Sure enough, they caught up with him in the bedroom, slashing her mattress. Ritch took the chair leg off Muff and tapped on the door.

'Didn't I say stay outside?' Ice snarled, spinning around.

Ritch smacked the knife out of his hand. It flew under the wardrobe. Ice's eyes narrowed to nothing. You never saw a kid turn that shifty so fast.

'What're you doing here?' he growled, then backed away.

The septic tattoo on his neck had leaked pus on his shirt.

Ritch said, 'The word is you wanna talk to me.'

Ice curled a lip but didn't say anything. Ritch gave the chair leg to Kenny and held his arms wide.

'OK, here I am. Fire away.' He didn't need any club.

Ice kept backing off till he stood in the corner.

'Not such a tough guy now, is he?' taunted Kenny. 'Not such a big man.'

Ritch grabbed Ice by the front of his leather jacket and bounced him hard off the wall. The louse launched a head butt but missed by a foot.

'He's scared stiff, look at him,' Kenny sneered as Ritch pushed Ice twice more. 'I'll bet he's wetting his pants.'

G said, 'C'mon now. Go easy,' and tried getting between them.

'Easy? Easy?' Muff laughed but not like something was funny. 'He said he wants to carve up your buddy.'

Ritch bounced Ice again. 'You little snake, this is long overdue,' he said through gritted teeth.

Ice covered up fast. The thug was outgunned. He needn't have worried, a gang beating wasn't what Ritch had in mind.

'This is between you and me, Ice,' he promised. 'You win and you walk. Ain't that right, fellas?'

'Whatever you say.' Muff hung over his shoulder

and didn't move very far.

Ice held his guard high. Slippery as ever, the creep refused to play ball.

Still he leered, 'As if,' and told Ritch what he could do to himself. Nothing original, the same tired old stuff.

If he doesn't trust me that's his stupid problem, Ritch thought. Maybe he ought to go ahead and bust him up anyway. The rat had it coming. And he was keen to oblige. Maggie's place was a wreck. Ice had wrenched out all the drawers and tossed her clothes everywhere. Old-style underwear and stockings lay strewn all around.

Near Ritch's feet a pink floral apron was tangled up with some blouses.

He got an idea. Ice was going to fight him for sure. Make no mistake.

'Put that on.'

He threw the apron at Ice. Automatically the yob caught it, then dropped it. He sneaked a look at the wardrobe. He really pined for that blade.

Ritch poked him one in the guts.

'Pick it up.'

He didn't budge. Ritch poked him again.

'Put it on.'

That didn't work, so he hit him much harder.

'Do it.'

Slowly Ice ducked his shaved head through the apron. The room filled with laughter and his bloodshot eyes burned with hate.

Ritch said, 'Now ain't that sweet? He wants to play house,' and looked around the room at the mess.

Muff tied off the apron strings. Kenny took a few practice swats with the chair leg. Ice cleared up the foam from the mattress and righted the drawers. Then he folded Maggie's clothes carefully and put them away.

Next, they wheeled him into the living room. Muff put an old dust-cap on Ice's head. Kenny said he wished that he had a camera. The skinhead spat at him but missed. The gobbet slid down the wall. Except for G they all blew Ice a kiss.

G said, 'This isn't good, Ritch. It's not funny.'

'It ain't supposed to be.' He ached to fight the guy.

'The point is to needle the jerk. Jeez, can't you see that?'

The ache had been burning him up for more than eight weeks.

G shrugged. He fetched the TV and toaster in from the garden. What more could he do? Muff dug out a vacuum cleaner, plugged it in and made Ice push it around. But Maggie had neighbours. Maybe he was getting a little carried away.

'What do you say now, hard man? Do we get it on?' Ritch offered Ice out one more time.

Sure the creep hated them. They all copped a bad-mouthing. Forget it though – no way would he bite. They kept him there anyway. He had to put the bungalow straight...

'What was that?' Kenny cocked an ear to the garden.

Ritch wasn't sure with all the row from the vacuum. It could be Maggie, or Ice's chicken-heart buddies back with the gang.

'Switch off, Muff.'

He slid to the window. A blue uniform straddled the high fence and then toppled in.

As they shot out the front way a patrol car screamed down the road at them. The doors flew open and two cops hit the ground running fast. A lightweight and a heavy. The last Ritch saw of Ice, he had the smaller guy on his tail.

The bigger guy was on his. Ritch raced past the bungalows, hung a left and scrambled over the garages. Boy, he really left that puffing flatfoot for dead.

When he got to his feet in the car park he saw a fourth cop, by the Alpha. Faking mild interest, Ritch strolled on by.

'Here, you. Not so fast.'

The cop looked young and fit. Ritch carried on walking.

'I said, come here.'

Ritch picked up speed.

'That means you.'

The cop quit radioing for the vehicle check and started towards him. Without looking back Ritch had it away on his toes. The cop flung down his helmet and got off his mark.

That cop was in the wrong job. He should have been sprinting for England.

Ritch hurdled some railings and swerved through

the playground, heading for a high-rise on the far side of the flats. Just before he got there he felt his right calf start to lock. Damn it. Cramp. Although he was in agony Ritch put on a spurt.

Vandals had kicked the lobby door off its hinges. The lift stood open and empty, reeking of puke. Maybe it worked, maybe not. Cornered, with no other choice, he reeled inside and punched 16 for the top.

The door shuddered but stayed open. He whacked the button again.

'Come on, come on.'

Nothing happened.

The cop sprinted into the lobby as the lift began closing. He dived for the gap and made a grab at the door. Ritch added his weight to its momentum. The lift shut and moved off.

'So long, sucker.' He laughed out loud.

Then he heard the copper race for the stairs.

Balancing on the lift handrail Ritch reached for the ceiling. After a struggle the access panel slid open wide. They were meant to have bolts in, that was the theory, but some clown or other always went round breaking them out. Ritch hauled himself up and squeezed through the gap. Panting and shaking he closed the panel, hitching a ride to the switch room up on the roof.

Soon his night vision improved. He counted the floors going past. By the tenth he couldn't see bottom. Not that it moved him, the old buzz wasn't there.

The lift ran straight to the top. Through the gloom he saw that the council had tried something new to screw up the vandals. Above his head a steel grid crossed the shaft, barring the exit. And it had a chain wrapped around it as thick as your wrist.

Ritch sat tight in the darkness.

His mind raced. If the cops caught him they'd throw the book at him. The Alpha, the bungalow. Whatever they had. The lift motor clicked and whirred and the car glided downward...

At the bottom two cops boarded.

Ritch heard their radios squawking, then the athlete said, 'Is that sealed, do you reckon?' The sap was still raring to go.

'It ought to be. Yeah,' a deeper voice said.

The panel moved under Ritch. He braced himself against the sides of the shaft and wished that he weighed twice as much.

'You're right.' The track star gave up pushing.

If the heavy had tried too Ritch would have been dead. The car jerked and they all moved off together. Nice and cosy, except that Ritch couldn't relax until the cops checked out each floor.

Four flats to a landing, they rang every doorbell. Soon Ritch's legs felt rigor mortised. Most of the tenants were out, though, and eventually the lift returned to the ground.

The cops split. Silence. Ritch rubbed his calf. Opting for safety for once, he stayed where he was.

Every so often the lift took off, up or down. Ritch sat in the dark and brooded about Alex. If he got caught, would she believe the cops' story? Or his?

In any case, chivvying Ice around, hanging out with kids like Kenny and Muff – that wasn't exactly going to turn him into her hero. Are you kidding? The way she hated violence? Her old man must have been beaten up by a burglar some time or other, that's how Ritch figured it.

From today, one certainty ruled: sooner or later Ice would take his revenge. Bet your sweet life. They were locked in a feud only one person would win.

Not having a date for a month had been murder.

Now this had to happen. He was dying to see her. It was driving him nuts.

His best pal would claim that he'd flipped, acting crazy over a girl. For such a quiet guy G had the scene sussed. But just round the corner there could be an Alex for him.

How Ritch saw things, going for somebody big-time wasn't like getting a pension. You couldn't plan for those feelings, or know what to do when they came. And most of all, getting knocked through a loop didn't take twenty-five years.

You're too young... It's too soon... You don't know each other.

He thought, what a crock. Love ain't a science. You can't calculate a formula to fit that kind of stuff.

The lift lurched off on another trip, a family going up to the fifth floor: two snivelling kids with their mum shouting and belting them. One trip too many for Ritch. As soon as they left he climbed out and then hit the stairs. Down on the ground floor the place was cop free.

Over at G's no one was home, either that or his old man wouldn't answer, so for a while Ritch hustled small change for a beer outside the shop. All the time he was hoping that he'd score another date with Alex real soon. Missing her hurt. A thousand times worse than cracking a rib or getting cramp in your calf.

He burst out laughing, the whole tears-in-the-eyes bit. Out loud he said, 'You sad sonofagun. Have you got it bad.'

Dead right. He shuffled home wondering whether that super-fit cop would be able to finger him. And if the guy did, and he got busted, would Alex stand by him? Or... ? Round and round, over and over.

The poor kid was in torment. Just like Billy had said.

part three

The school year was over. At first that didn't mean much to Ritch. After half an hour in the dole office he became a Youth Training Scheme dropout. Signing on as a wage slave didn't really appeal to him. So he told them to stick their benefit where the sun doesn't shine...

'It's too hot in here,' Alex complained and fanned herself with a hardback *Tess of the D'Urbervilles*. Then she rolled on to her stomach and started studying again. Holiday or not, the girl was keeping right at it.

Ritch said, 'What d'you expect? It's too darn hot everywhere.'

They were stretched out on the floor in his room trying not to boil over. The weather burned hotter than a Miami heatwave. The flat felt like a sauna. Traffic fumes blew in the window. Outside, a car horn sounded too long and too loud.

'Shall I switch the fan on?' Ritch dropped the *Shoot!* he'd been browsing through.

'Don't be a tease.'

Fair enough, the flat didn't own one. Alex took a break. Her face shone with sweat.

'I will have a tall glass of iced tea, though, please.'

'OK,' he said. 'After this.'

Soon as they'd arrived she'd changed into her swimsuit, a two-piecer. Ritch blew on her neck then her back and her skin got goosebumps.

'Mmm, that feels good.'

She looked as fine as any surfer girl on Waikiki beach. They had the flat to themselves. Ritch's old lady and the Jerk were out, down at the Cowshed. That was the one good thing about Gerry, he wouldn't stay in at all. Not while the old lady had a pound or two left in her purse.

'This side's dry.' Ritch leaned back.

'Don't stop. It feels marvellous.'

'Turn over, then.'

He blew on her face and she closed her eyes.

They'd been seeing more of each other since her gran had come back from Eastbourne. A date every week or so, more or less.

Alex tilted her head.

'Kiss,' she demanded.

Ritch kissed her lips and then carried on blowing.

Life can be weird. More ups and downs than a white-knuckle fairground ride. Three months before, in the lift shaft, he'd been worried sick over their future.

Now, except for the weather, everything was cool.

They'd seen plenty of movies and won a few more quid at the dogs. And nothing had happened after the break-in at Maggie Finn's bungalow. At least not to Ritch.

'How about this?'

'Don't you dare!'

She hated having her navel touched. He dried the last beads of sweat on her forehead instead.

Ice had got collared but they let him off with a caution. He wore someone's school uniform to court; his old lady most likely cried. Who cared? Anyway, the blood feud between them still stood, and Ritch hadn't told Al.

'That was lovely.' She shivered and sat up. 'Now, where's that tea?'

'How do you make it?' He played dumb.

'With tea and ice, silly.'

She whacked Ritch with the pillow, slipped his shirt on and padded off to the bathroom in her bare feet. A tower block overlooked the hall window. She was the kind of girl who kept her T-shirt on if there were guys at the beach.

The relaxed way she walked knocked Ritch out.

The best part was that she didn't realise she was doing it. Natural. Totally natural. He went in the kitchen and filled the kettle right to the brim.

Ritch cleared up the cartons from Gerry's tandoori. The Jerk had been out with the boys the night before. At least that's what he claimed.

The kettle took a long time to boil so Ritch sneaked back on Alex. She was chewing her nails, well lost in thought.

'Didn't your mother ever warn you about getting bad habits?'

He straddled her waist, gripping her wrists.

'Look who's talking.' She raised her eyes to the ceiling. 'I don't complain when you crack your knuckles.'

'Who does?'

'You do, when you're reading.' With a twist of her hips she threw the clown off.

He mussed up her hair. A police siren wailed by down on the main stem. The hot weather was keeping them busy. It had everyone steamed up and on edge.

Well, almost everyone. Ritch said, 'What if I do? Admit it, you're crazy about me.'

'I think you must mean mad to put up with you.'

She rolled away and puffed out her cheeks.

'Are they getting on at you again?' he probed.

Although Clare refused to back her up any more, Alex had told her parents that she was visiting her cousin. So far the plan to deceive them was working out fine.

'Are they?'

She had to be home before nine. Ritch was keeping an eye on the clock. He'd set the alarm for half eight to be safe but the thing didn't work so good since he'd bowled it at the wall one time too many. Those early Saturdays were frying his brain.

'Come on, are they?'

She groaned. 'I was thinking about next year and uni. That's all.'

After her A-levels next summer she had three more years left to get to her goal.

'Why bother going?' he said. 'Chewing broken glass would be more entertaining.'

'I've explained, I don't know how many times, that I want to teach.'

The way she said it you had to believe her.

'Are your grades slipping?'

'Of course not.' She didn't pretend to be average. 'Can we drop the subject now?'

She could purr at you one minute and then claw you the next. Ritch clammed up and thumbed through her notes on *Tess of the D'Urbervilles*. The stuff in there in Alex's neat italic made this farm girl seem like a real wimp...

After a while he said, 'How's your granny these days?'

'Very well, thank you.'

The old woman was Alex's grandmother on her old lady's side. Eighty years old, she got by on her own with four cats and a budgie for company. During her husband's lifetime they'd gone to Nepal to climb mountains. Ritch had never met her but she sounded tough. Just like her grand-kid.

'Has she made up her mind?' he asked.

Alex didn't say anything.

'Is it gonna be cremation or burial?'

'Don't be so horrid.' She punched his arm.

It was a long-running discussion they had. Old people normally have that whole deal figured out.

He was always asking about the old woman's plans.

He said, 'Cremation's quicker and cleaner. None of that hanging about at the graveside, lowering away.'

'And I suppose you'll want me to look after your ashes when you have it done?'

She screwed up her face, feigning disgust.

'Nope. You get to scatter them.'

'Where?' she asked. He had her interest now.

'I ain't fussy. How about on your old man's front lawn, so I can come back to haunt him?'

'I thought that you didn't believe in life after death?'

'In my case I'll make an exception.'

'How altruistic.'

'That's my middle name.' He didn't know what she meant. It was worth playing the fool, though, to conjure that smile. 'What do you reckon?'

Alex gave it some thought. 'I'd like a marble sarcophagus carved all over with cats.'

Sometimes she said left on a hillside, like the native Americans. The kettle was whistling.

'Very exotic.' Ritch got up. 'It better be airtight, 'cos I won't come to see you if you start to smell bad.'

'You horrible pig.'

Without putting on his shirt she chased him into the kitchen.

They wrestled around for a while. Then he fixed the iced tea while Alex made them a salad from a limp head of lettuce and a pair of boiled eggs. Swapping favourite movies, they ate supper there.

Afterwards, they washed up the plates stacked in the sink, like an old married couple. Then Ritch brought the jug of tea and they went back to his room to play draughts. Someone had left a travel set on Billy's train a few leaves ago.

Ritch was just about average but Alex was expert – chess was her usual game. She beat him three games straight and then let him win. He could always tell. When she took a dive the girl blushed like wildfire.

'Best of seven?' he kidded.

'You're such a glutton for punishment. Don't you know when you're beaten?'

'Yeah – never,' he grinned.

Ritch poured out the last of the tea. She pressed the cold glass to her cheek. He imagined it hissing. The girl really killed him. If she ever learned poker he'd leave her flat broke.

Study break was over. *Tess* reappeared, along with the highlight pen. Ritch read about a new scheme to catch football stars of the future at an even earlier age...

Alex quit studying and gnawed at her fingers. Tearing away, she sighed and then turned on her side. With her eyes boring into him Ritch read the same sentence three times in a row.

'All right.' He gave up and put the magazine down. 'I surrender. If it's not your parents, or grades, what's up? What's the big problem?'

'I'm awfully worried, Ritch.'

'What about?' It wasn't like her to hedge.

'You and me.'

'How do you mean? We're doing great.'

'We are now. But what will happen when I go up to Cambridge?'

He hadn't thought that far ahead. He never did.

'You're bound to meet someone new.' Before Ritch could deny it she went on, 'Or if you don't, I certainly will.'

She had a point. The place was going to be crawling

with hotshot intellectuals and high-flying career guys. Ritch couldn't see Alex's parents chasing them off. The red carpet would get rolled out in a hurry. Hell, Alex might even find a boy wonder she liked.

They'd never made plans and Ritch hated to rush this. He had to gamble, though, so he pressed on.

'Suppose I come along for the ride?'

Suddenly she went poker-faced on him. He couldn't read her. Then she was the one rushing to clear every fence.

'I doubt that we'll get a flat on my paltry loan.' But at least they'd escape... 'We may have to share with some freshers. Cambridge can be very expensive. And sometimes my father can be a mite close with his cash.'

A mite close? The man locked his drinks cabinet, for crying out loud.

'I'll take a job slinging burgers,' Ritch boasted. 'Or jockeying pizza. Even Cambridge eggheads eat junk food, I'll bet.'

'In that case perhaps we could manage a bed-sit. We shouldn't try to run before we're able to walk.'

'Why not? I always do.'

'Yes. It's a habit that you'll have to break, I'm

afraid.' Alex kissed his mouth softly. 'We both have to work at this, Ritch. I need to get my degree. Some day I'm going to teach.'

He told her that he'd rather stand in front of a charging rhino than get in her way. They both thought things over. It was a big step.

'I'll be studying most of the time. We may have to stay in a lot.' She doubted he could. 'You're bound to get bored.'

'Oh yeah?' Ritch kissed her, strong.

'You will,' she insisted.

'If I get suicidal I can always go watch Cambridge United.' In the bottom division – he laughed at the joke. 'In any case, once I land a job, maybe I can take up night classes...'

'Perhaps there's a course in zoology, something vocational that applies to a vet.' She was way, way ahead of him.

'Right. With some kind of practical work.'

'If you volunteer to help out at a clinic like the Blue Cross, who knows where it might lead?'

They thought it over some more.

Alex put her head on his shoulder. 'We might have trouble finding a landlord who takes pets.'

Thomas, her cat.

'Nah, we'll hide him. No worries.' He stroked her hair.

'After the first year perhaps we could rent an unfurnished room.'

'Great. You pick out the wallpaper and I'll paste it up.'

Before the guy had run out, Ritch used to help his old man with the odd moonlighting job. His dad was a painter and decorator, a tosher, by trade.

Outside, there was the crump of windscreen glass breaking. A car alarm shrieked. Ritch said, 'I can't believe that I'm finally gonna bale out of this hole.'

Alex snuggled tighter. 'Won't your mother be upset about losing you?'

'She won't hardly notice.'

At last he explained about the non-stop fights, the old man leaving home, the old lady's long string of boyfriends. It felt good to get the whole rotten mess off his chest.

'They sound completely ill-suited.' Alex dug her fingers into his arm. She was shocked. 'Why on earth would they marry?'

'Could be it was only a physical thing,' Ritch took

a wild guess. 'Anyway, they both wound up hitched to the wrong person.'

For too many hours in this dump of a flat.

'It must have been awful.'

'It had its moments.'

She hunched her shoulders.

'Do you think we'll end up like that? Always quarrelling? Hating each other?'

'A top wildlife vet and some big English professor? Are you kidding?'

He massaged her back.

'We'll be OK, Alex. We're not like them.'

Like two kids planning Christmas in November they talked till they slept.

The alarm clattered at a quarter past nine. The pair got dressed in a blur. Running over to her house, Alex made Ritch vow no more fights, no more aggro.

'Who, me?' he panted.

'I mean it, Ritch. Or you can forget about Cambridge.'

'OK.'

'Ritch.'

'All right. I swear it.' She was as relentless as a glacier flowing downhill.

*

No one ever hung out in the Village. The streets were all empty. Everywhere, the air-conditioning was going full blast. The young lovers didn't quit running till they reached her front gate. Even so Alex's curfew was totally blown.

'Shall I come in with you?' Ritch volunteered.

'Not unless you want to die young.'

She quickly kissed him goodbye.

'Don't fret, I'll survive,' she said. 'I usually do.'

He stuck around anyway behind his usual tree. Alex's people were really messed up. They didn't deserve her. They've got a life, he thought. Why can't they let her off the leash?

Inside the house someone began shouting. Ritch crossed the lawn and swarmed up the drainpipe next to the garage. As he made its flat roof a van drew up at the kerb.

He plunged down behind the raised guttering. A rentacop in a brown uniform got out and played his torch over the garage. Ritch pressed his cheek against the soft tar on the roof.

The way the guy slogged up the driveway every

burglar in the neighbourhood must have heard his boots crunch.

Ritch took a deep breath and got ready to jump.

The geek rattled the padlock, scratched his butt and then fired up a cigarette. Coughing the whole way, he slouched back to the van.

For a while the security guard sat there and excavated one nostril. No wonder the sap works alone, Ritch thought with a grin.

Pretty soon the crime-busting charmer drove off. Behind Ritch, Alex's study lamp clicked on. She flopped in the swivel chair, facing into the room, and he reached up and tapped on the pane.

She gave a start then spun round, saw him and poked out her tongue.

As she was raising the window he hissed, 'Turn that flipping light out.'

'Aren't you supposed to say, "What light through yonder window breaks?"' she whispered and smiled.

The quotation flew right over his head. Once she'd doused the lamp he asked, 'Did they suss us out?'

'Not for a second. Don't look so worried.'

'I heard them rucking at you.'

'Oh, that's nothing.'

It hadn't sounded that way to Ritch.

'Actually they were in quite a good mood,' she soothed. 'Their bridge party went rather well.'

'What are they like on a bad night?' he asked, and she smiled again.

But he was serious. 'We should talk to them. One night they might get round to calling on Clare.'

'I don't want to hurt them.' Her outstretched hand didn't quite reach down to his. 'And I've told you before, this way we win.'

'But...'

'It's best my way. Trust me.' She had her parents utterly fooled.

Suddenly Alex touched a finger to her lips. Her mother was moving about on the ground floor, switching off lights. Her father put out the cat. Have it your way, Ritch thought. She must know her own people. Obviously, no one had told the poor stiff how *Romeo and Juliet* ends.

Before they could talk any more they both heard them coming upstairs. So he whispered goodnight and got out of there fast.

*

All over the estate families were sitting out on their doorsteps. Near the flats a bunch of girls were horsing around lobbing water balloons high in the air. Not up for a drenching, Ritch crossed the street.

Along by the Cowshed a crowd of drinkers had spilled onto the pavement. The sight of all those cold pints of lager made his throat ache.

Broke as usual, he wandered down to the sheds.

Two junior winos who worked at the car wash were there, splitting a bottle of fortified wine. Electric soup. All three played cards and talked about motors. By the time they cracked their second bottle Ritch decided to split. That high-octane hooch could do your head in.

Cheap booze can also make for a mean drunk. Not me, Ritch bragged. Not this time. He was walking on air.

Together with Alex, he was aiming for Cambridge. In a little over a year they'd have their own room. She'd be dazzling her tutors, or whatever you called them. Ritch would be working with animals. Maybe only cats, not lions or tigers. But he'd get there some day. The lucky pair had it all. They were on their way to the top.

He was wondering whether to apply for night classes right now, right away, when he cut through the alley. Something exploded at the back of his skull. The sucker-punched kid went down as if he was dead.

Ritch tried to stand up. No chance. A boot smashed into his ribs and someone stomped both his hands.

Ice said, 'Let's see how cool you shoot pool now, champ,' and sniggered into his face.

The rat stank of glue. For good measure he sliced Ritch's ear. After that they all kicked him around like he was a football. He curled up tight and attempted to roll with it. All he wanted was for the pain to leave off.

When they'd had enough – maybe they got bored or just plain tired – they swaggered off, laughing and joking.

Hurting bad, Ritch dragged himself to his feet.

There were five of them. Ice bounced along wiping his bloody hand on his sleeve.

Ritch yelled, 'Come on, then. How d'you fancy it? One at a time? All together?'

They swung round to face him. Staggering, then running, the crazy fool steamed into the pack.

*

The motorway pile-up must have been bad. As the firemen were dragging Ritch out of the wreckage they burned his leg with the cutting torch. He screamed at the idiot to take more care. The fire-fighter's face transmorphed into Alex's and she whispered, 'It's too late for that, Ritch. Much, much, much too late.'

He woke well adrift. The sheets were too tight and some joker had stuffed the pillow with kerbstones. He moved his head. Sunlight shone between the slats of a dusty grey blind. This room was small. Ritch's was the only bed in it. For one long second he didn't remember. Then the cop in the chair by the door slid into view and it all flooded back.

Some concerned citizen had phoned for an ambulance but the Law showed up too. At the hospital a doctor X-rayed Ritch, stitched him, then doped him up. The cops asked to interview him. The way Ritch was banged up, the doctor refused.

The Law said, no sweat, they were going round to see his old lady. He didn't waste his breath telling them she'd gone down the pub.

They promised to send someone over with her to chat with Ritch the next day. Here the cop was, bright and early. At least the heatwave had broken. It was hot, though nothing to write home about, not like before.

The cop stood by the bed and said, 'Good morning, Richard,' as if being polite to a tearaway gave him heartburn.

'The name's Ritch. What's good about it?' His stitches were on fire.

The Law's mouth cracked in a smile.

'I take your point. You're in quite a fix, aren't you?'

He was an old beat cop, too dim to make sergeant, yet the sap really thought that he knew the score. There was no sign of Ritch's old lady. That figured. It was par for the course.

The know-all in blue kept up his smile while he read from his notebook.

'According to our information you have some bruising round your lungs, six stitches in your ear, a cracked shin and three broken fingers.'

Ice had been thorough.

'Right.' The cop let the smile fade. 'Do you know who attacked you?'

Ritch shook his head. 'Everything's blank.'

Some time in the future he intended paying Ice a visit. And he wouldn't need any help from an old dead-beat like this.

'No idea at all?'

'Zilch. It was dark. They surprised me.'

'How unfortunate.'

Most likely he lived out in some leafy suburb.

'Can you give me a description? Height, weight or age?'

'I didn't see anything.'

'How many of them were there? Three? Four? Twenty?'

Now the guy was trying to be smart.

Ritch said, 'If I'd have known you were this interested I'd have booked you a seat at the ringside.'

After that he got the message, gave up and left.

Breakfast arrived, coffee and a poached egg on toast. It smelled good but Ritch couldn't eat it. His face hurt too much. What doesn't? he thought. A different nurse came on duty. She rolled the blind up. The sun had climbed high in the sky. Ritch swallowed the pain-killers the nurse gave him and then nodded out.

Later on, the doctor who'd put off the cops stopped by to see him.

'You ought to select your next opponent within your own weight division, old chap,' he drawled, checking the bruises.

Pure public school, yet he had a nose like a boxer who'd had one fight too many. From the size of his frame he probably played rugby in the front row.

Ritch said, 'You ain't seen the other kid,' as if he'd massacred somebody.

The doc fixed up a stethoscope and tuned in to his lungs. 'Sometimes being too game isn't wise. Knives can kill. I know, I've seen it.'

'At least if you're dead you can't feel any pain, can you?' Ritch joked.

'No one your age should talk that way.' The pug's forehead creased like an old road map. 'You must be bored in here. I'll try to round up a spare TV set somewhere.'

'Thanks.'

'I'm afraid that this was the only bed that we had.'

'I'm fine. I like my own company.'

For one of the 'chaps' he wasn't so bad. The accent set your teeth on edge but that wasn't his fault. Ritch thought, at least he told the Law where to go. And it was only a lottery what parents you got stuck with, or where you'd been born.

At lunch Ritch couldn't even handle the soup. His ear really throbbed, he just toyed with the spoon.

They cleared away the plates and he fell asleep watching an old crime series on the black-and-white portable they brought him. The reception was terrible but, so what, the programme was too.

When he surfaced he had a visitor. G copped a close look at Ritch's face and then pulled up a chair. He'd brought a bulging carrier-bag with him.

'Gross,' he complained. 'What was he packing? A chainsaw or something?'

'Thanks a million.' Ritch tried to grin but the stitches tugged hard in the opposite direction. 'You should try it from this side. It ain't exactly a ball.'

His visitor winced at the thought.

'How did you find out?' Ritch wanted to know.

'Bad news travels fast.'

Especially with a loudmouth like Ice to broadcast it round.

G dropped the bag by the bed, frowned and said, 'What happened, wild ass? What did you do?'

Seemed like everyone was standing in for Ritch's old man that afternoon.

He ran through the details, including a damage report. At the time he didn't realise that things were going to get a lot worse.

'You really taught them a lesson,' G said when Ritch finished. 'Anyone can see that.'

He could have said, I told you so, too. But he didn't. He was biding his time.

'Do you reckon those two wine connoisseurs set me up?' Ritch asked, almost convinced.

'Are you paranoid?' His pal looked at him as if he'd gone loco. 'Ice is a chancer. He saw an opportunity to get even and jumped in. That's all.'

'I'll make the creep jump all right.'

'Then it'll be your turn again. That's how it works. Revenge is strictly for losers.'

G stared right at Ritch, hard.

'I ain't no loser,' the invalid complained.

'Right now I wouldn't bet on that, ole buddy.'

All the years that Ritch had known the kid they'd never seen eye to eye about violence. Yet they were still tight, more like brothers than friends. So he let the dig pass.

Instead he said, 'Wanna fight?' and put up both bandaged fists.

'Here. They're mostly autobiographies.' G dumped the carrier-bag on the end of the bed, took off his glasses and cleaned a smear off the lens.

A slick of paperbacks and hardbacks spilled over the sheets. The spines were uncracked, they looked almost brand new. At least twenty-five books about sports packed into one bulging sack.

'Nice work. Where did you hoist them?' Ritch asked, winding him up.

G put his glasses back on and glared at the clown. 'You know that bookstore in the Village?'

'The one where the security guard's got a white stick?'

'They've hired this new Saturday girl.' His pal sighed. 'She lets me have the review copies once they've finished reading them.'

'And?'

'Roddy Doyle is her favourite writer.'

Who's he? Ritch thought, but stayed quiet, holding out to hear more.

'She wears purple all the time, collects soda-siphons and anything else with chrome on it. She's an artist...'

The smile spread across Ritch's face. Then the stitches bit deeper. G's glare grew meaner and Ritch held up his hands.

'Whoa, I didn't say anything. I'll bet she's terrific.'

He waited a second before following through. 'Would she have a set of hub-caps to fit an old Escort, d'you reckon?'

G let it ride. He couldn't get more brassed off with Ritch than he felt already. The nurse came in with another cup of pain-killers. Grateful, Ritch washed them down. He hoped they weren't the kind of junk that might get you hooked.

G asked if he needed anything brought up at all. Ritch said, 'Not many. Bake me a cake with a file inside.' Before he could stop himself he yawned, gaping wide.

'Sleep's the only place you're going, son,' his buddy crowed.

He didn't hear Ritch arguing. Last night hadn't exactly been crammed end to end with quality sack time. G repacked the carrier-bag and wedged the books under the bed. Ritch's eyelids felt heavier than the biggest crate on Big Tony's stall.

His visitor got up to go. 'I'd better be leaving. They said not to tire you.'

Ritch asked him to let his old lady know where she could find him.

'No worries.' He ruffled Ritch's hair. 'I'll see you tomorrow. Try not to pick a fight with the doctor between now and then.'

Ritch said, 'Have you seen the gorilla?'

G nodded. 'I wouldn't go chasing the nurses.'

'Funny. Real funny, pal.'

The scholar stopped at the door.

'Which reminds me. I bumped into your pen-pal this morning. She came over here with me, and sent me in first.'

Jesus. Alex.

'Poor girl.' G whistled through his teeth. 'Have you looked in the mirror yet?'

Which reminds him, Ritch thought. Yeah, right...Like fun it did.

As his first visitor was leaving, Ritch saw Alex sitting outside, reading a magazine. Her jaw was set tight. G was right. If he stood in front of a mirror it would most likely crack. Right now that seemed the least of his problems though. The very least.

Alex shut the door and stood with her back to it. Her unblinking stare cut him straight to the bone.

Ritch couldn't hack the silence. He muttered, 'It wasn't my fault,' and then her stack blew. With both fists clenched she flew to the bedside.

'Do you expect me to believe that?' she started yelling. 'Do you? Because I really can't see how you can believe it yourself.'

One of the nurses looked in and asked if anything was wrong. Ritch mumbled, 'I'm fine.' Alex blushed and said, 'Hi.' The nurse ducked back out but left the door open.

Ritch rubbed his leg where the plaster was chafing.

'They jumped me,' he reasoned.

'I don't want to hear about your macho vendetta. You promised me, didn't you?'

She stamped her foot.

'You lied to me, Ritch.'

That hurt worse than the rucking. He felt pretty

lousy. Alex ran rings round her parents – but she'd always told him the truth.

'That rat started it all.'

This time she muted her voice.

'I've never met a boy so pigheaded, so selfish…'

In a low-key way it was a four-star tongue lashing. Ritch'd had a long day, the pills were knocking him sideways. He fought to keep his eyes open and, at last, Alex ran out of steam. Wiping her nose with a tissue she glanced out of the window, back at Ritch, then out of the window again.

'Does it hurt very badly?' The hothead looked really sick.

Still tight-lipped she reached out to examine his stitches. At the last second her shaking fingers stopped an inch from his face.

'Will you have a scar?'

'Could be.' Ice's knife was serrated. 'We can tell…' Ritch wanted to say, everyone we meet up at Cambridge. 'You can say that I ran into your squash racket some time.'

'I don't play squash.'

Nice try. No cigar. Suddenly Alex sat down and rummaged around in her shoulder-bag. With her face hidden from view she blew her nose.

'I've brought some things for you.'

Her voice sounded thick, like she was getting a head cold. When she straightened up, her eyes looked puffy and red. Muzzy with drugs, Ritch thought, she should be in bed too.

'Here – three kinds of fruit, a draughts set, and you won't have read this.'

A book about hand-rearing lion cubs.

'Gee, thanks. I saw the movie—'

'It's a textbook, actually.' She'd swung back in control.

'Oh yeah, right. I'll take notes.'

'If your promises were worth anything we wouldn't be here.'

A yawn almost ripped the stitches out of his face. At this rate, he panicked, she won't even think that you care.

But Alex said, 'You're worn out, aren't you? I ought to leave.'

'Wait. Stay a bit longer.'

Ritch laid his hand on her arm. The doctor hadn't skimped on the bandages. The girl took one look at his knuckles then sat back down.

There was a fruit bowl in the cabinet. Arranging the grapes, pears and peaches as if they were flowers, Alex said, brightening her voice, 'Your friend Geoff's awfully sweet, isn't he?'

'Awfully.' Ritch couldn't wait to lay that gem on his buddy.

'We were in the same bookshop this morning.'

She put a grape in his mouth. The juice stung his bust lip.

'I had Clare with me so he probably felt rather awkward.'

The way she peered at Ritch he wasn't going to like what came next.

'Geoff thinks if you don't quit this imbecile vendetta it's bound to destroy you.'

'He's worse than my old—'

'Granny? Oh no, I don't believe so. He's very acute.'

Alex was trying to say, it's your life or death.

With G backing her up Ritch didn't burn energy arguing. Those pain-killing pills were knocking him out...

Alex set up the draughtboard on his bedside table. Now that her final point had been scored she wanted to play. He called out instructions, she shifted the pieces and checked out his face every now and again. Her cold must have been gaining because she kept blowing her nose.

Groggy as hell Ritch won three games in a row.

'What are you smiling at?' Alex lined them up for a fourth game. 'I can't see anything funny. Are you feeling OK?'

'Terrific. The stitches are itchy, that's all.'

But he closed his eyes.

'If it's OK with you I'll give this one a miss.' His voice trailed away.

'You're shattered, aren't you?' She was annoyed not to have noticed. 'Tell me the truth.'

Ritch thought, for a change?

'A crack or two, maybe. But shattered? Not me.'

The blood began pounding loud in his ears. Alex's voice came from a distance, as if she was the one passing out.

Ritch heard her packing the draughts set away in the cabinet. The nurse bustled through and made a fuss about him needing to rest. Alex took the broad hint.

Her lips brushed his forehead.

'I'll leave the board there. Perhaps you can find someone to play.'

Ritch tried to say, 'Are we still on for Cambridge next year?' but his own lips had gone numb. Those lousy downers. Feeling the pain would have been better. He didn't even hear Alex finish saying goodbye. While he was sleeping the girl slipped away.

Ritch's old lady was drawing the dole. Naturally he hadn't let on to the Law where she worked. G went round to the flat and left a message with Gerry. Of course that lazy rat would never hike to a phone.

The sun was setting when his mum finally arrived.

'You've always been nothing but trouble,' were the first words out of her mouth.

Her eyes looked really bloodshot. She'd had a good time in the boozer the evening before. This late, the effects of the hangover were still hanging on. It showed in the lines on her face. She ain't twenty no more, Ritch thought. By now you'd think that she'd learn.

He'd only been awake a few minutes. Half

doped, half drowsing, he watched the sunset and let her run off at the mouth...

Pretty soon his mum was saying, 'It's all my fault, baby,' her bottom lip trembling, spinning in circles like she couldn't decide.

Ritch said, 'Don't cry. Not here.'

He felt bad enough already. Seeing her face crumple made him depressed.

'How could you do this to your own mother?' she sobbed.

'I'm the one hurt here,' Ritch reminded her. 'Don't worry, I'll live.'

She always did love a drama, or a good soap.

The sunset changed from orange to crimson. The nurse on duty gave his old lady fifteen minutes more, a cup of tea and a tablet, then he sent her home.

Next morning Ritch crept to the phone in the hall, rang her at work and told her not to stop by again.

Worrying about Alex – their future uncertain – didn't he already have enough on his plate?

Over the next couple of days the quacks straightened his body out. They couldn't do much for his mind. Ritch was getting over-anxious to leave – Alex hadn't come back to visit him, though G did every night. Most of the time he just lay in bed aching to see her. When the poor stiff wasn't fretting, his ragged hopes soared.

If Alex gave him the chance he was definitely going to find work and learn about animals in Cambridge. Then, once she'd earned her degree, maybe they'd travel. Make a clean break, get away from it all. A year running around Europe like G had planned sounded good. They could do something seasonal to finance the trip. Fruit picking, that kind of game.

Living free on the road without any hassles would be good for them both after all that staying home, studying. Spain might be the right place to start – the Costa del Lager. Fun, sun, booze and beach parties. Plus, Barcelona had a great football team. The Nou Camp stadium looked fabulous... They'd see it all wherever they went.

Lying on that hospital mattress Ritch worked out his options. He didn't want to wind up like one of those sadsacks down at the Cowshed, with his own special corner. The time had come to wipe the slate clean and start over again. No more trouble. He really meant it. To hell with Ice and his gutless crew. Ritch's mind was made up. From now on he'd wise up and fly straight, not go on with the feud. He was determined – one thousand per cent.

At that point he came down with a cough. A real bad one, a monster. It made him hack the whole time. So they didn't discharge him, which was a drag. At least Ritch had his own room. They thought that if they moved him onto a ward he'd keep the others awake at night. That was the one small piece of luck that he got.

During one of his calls the doctor said Ritch had contracted a virus.

'I blame this dive of a mortuary.' Ritch loved baiting the rugger toff. 'I was healthy enough before you took me in here.'

The quack laughed. 'Appendectomies and hernias aren't very contagious. Don't worry, we only do minor surgery here – there's no Lassa fever, old chap.'

By then, if the doctor called Ritch that, he heard buddy or pal.

The doc was going to say something more but Ritch felt another fit of coughing erupting. When it was finished the guy took the bedside bowl off him and cleaned up the mess.

Ritch caught his breath and said, 'What price do I get on that hernia?' He'd almost busted a gut.

'I haven't lost a patient to one yet,' his pal joked. 'We'll soon have you up and about.'

Sure enough, he gave Ritch a course of pills that would have cured a worldwide flu epidemic. When the kid moved he rattled. For a couple of weeks the cough didn't budge though. He got pretty sick, and felt even sicker once they cancelled visiting hours. Then the infection dispersed. He copped the all-clear and on the Monday his mum ran him home.

Man, she looked rough. She wore her everyday work clothes and hadn't bothered with make-up. Normally she'd slap on mascara to pop down the shops.

Ritch slid in the back of the Escort, stretched out and put the walking stick that they'd loaned him on the rear ledge.

After a few blocks his old lady lit up her third cigarette, glanced at him in the mirror then plugged the lighter back in the dash.

'Gerry's gone,' she said. 'He cleared out yesterday morning.'

Ritch felt sorry enough for her. He guessed she had to have someone. If only she'd learn to be more selective. Anyway, the good news was the Jerk had moved out of the flat.

'The little skirt-chaser. He'll probably crawl back to his ex in Southampton.' His old lady steered the Escort into the car park.

Ritch got his walking stick ready.

'It's no loss, believe me,' he warned her.

Nor would her next one be, he'd have a bet.

Wrapped in a blanket Ritch sat out on the balcony. There was only room for two chairs and the satellite dish, but it had a great view of the motorway. He used to get a bang out of watching the joy-riders out-running the cops.

Every five minutes the old lady poked her head out of the kitchen and asked, 'Do you fancy a tea, love?' as if an overdose of caffeine would put everything right. Or she came and fussed with his blanket.

She was doing her best. It still drove Ritch crazy.

At last he said, 'Look, I feel terrific. You don't have to lose the whole morning. Why not go into work?'

She didn't get paid for taking time off. There was more chance of Ritch running a marathon. Moping around the place wouldn't help her get Gerry back, either. She needed plenty of company. That was her style.

She threw on some lipstick and left. The stream of traffic below slowed down then gridlocked. Most likely some moron had caused a shunt running up the slip road.

Soon the horns began blaring. Then they settled in for the wait. Without so much traffic it got kind of peaceful. The shouts of kids playing tag wafted up from the street down below. On the next floor above someone murdered a top twenty song.

The sky looked clear blue, like the Sunday Ritch and Alex had gone for their walk along by the towpath. It hurt to remember. No way could he stop himself though. He never could...

*

Alex said her parents would kill her if they ever found out. That part of the canal had a rep as the town's Lovers' Lane. Ritch didn't know why. He'd only ever seen people fishing or walking the dog there. Gossips love to have someone to run down, he guessed.

Out in the sticks they stopped for a drink at a pub by the lock. Ritch got Alex a real lemonade, made on the premises, plus a pint of rough cider for him.

The beer garden was crowded with families, so they went down to the water's edge. An old narrow houseboat was navigating the weir.

Alex waved to the woman on deck and called, 'Isn't that a beautiful lifestyle?' Then she smiled at Ritch.

'There'd be no one harassing us. We'd be totally free.'

Ritch took a gulp of his scrumpy, and shuddered. That stuff can strip the enamel right off your teeth.

'Free?' he said. 'Who'd pay the mooring fees?'

She chucked a segment of lemon, he ducked.

'Don't pretend to be cynical. That's only a pose that you hide behind.'

The lock filled with water and the boat slowly rose.

In the same breath Alex said, 'And when are you going to look for a job?' as if the two subjects were one.

'As soon as I get the time.' He avoided her eye.

'But you only work a few hours on Saturday morning.'

'Get out of here. I never stop, do I?'

'Snoring in bed all day? Getting into scrapes late at night?' She knew him too well.

'You're gonna make a great mother for some poor kid, someday,' Ritch laughed. The girl really would.

A coach full of day-trippers unloaded in front of the boozer. They all piled into the main bar making plenty of noise. That mob were going to have a ball no matter who they upset. Just passing through, why should they care?

Alex said, 'What have you got planned for next year?'

'Nothing.' She asked some weird questions. 'Same as the last, I expect. How about you?'

She counted to ten.

'If you're serious about being a vet there's a course—'

'I can't hack teachers,' he dived in, 'and they don't like me.'

'Listen to you not letting me finish. You're terrified that it might be too hard.'

'It's too late for me, anyhow.'

'Rubbish. I could teach you myself. We'd start with the basics at first. English and maths.'

That was Alex. She never gave up.

Ritch drained his glass and went to get the second one in. Alex's folks were driving Granny to a garden centre after their lunch. The old mountaineer lived across town and the centre was way out that side, so Alex didn't have to rush home for a change.

As he came out with the drinks she jumped straight at him. 'You'll never amount to anything unless you have the courage to fail.'

Ritch scowled at the sky.

'Don't keep on.' He held out her lemonade. 'Lighten up. Enjoy yourself...soak up the rays.'

Al turned her back to him. 'I just hate to see you throwing your life away.' She worried a lot.

He put down the drinks and went to spin her around, but she wouldn't budge.

'You're here then you ain't,' he argued. 'What's there to throw?'

'I see. Because life isn't infinite, you won't bother to try. You won't get off your haunches.'

Love has a flip side. She stormed off down the path.

Ritch thought, what's got into her now?

Every time he came close Alex sped further away. He couldn't work out what the heck had been bugging her, but Ritch kept his pride by refusing to run. Feeling an idiot, the kid trailed far behind.

At the top of her street Alex braked to a walking pace. He quickly caught up.

Before he could speak she said, 'Goodbye, Ritch.'

Meaning, so long.

Not believing his ears the poor sap stayed in step. At the gate he slid his arm round her waist and lunged for a kiss. Right there in broad daylight. He didn't care who saw any more. Alex shoved him away.

'Is that all I am? Something to paw at?'

That brassed him off totally.

'Could be. What do *you* think?'

Wham. She slapped his face hard and ran up the

path. But the key wouldn't fit in the lock. Without making a sound Alex started to cry.

At last she got the door open and flew up the stairs. Freaked out, Ritch raced up too.

Alex threw herself on the bed. Her shoulders were heaving, tears streamed down both cheeks. The scary thing was she still didn't make any noise.

Ritch's ear throbbed where the smack had crash-landed. He lay on the quilt anyway kissing her neck.

'Sorry, Al,' he said. 'I'm sorry.'

'No, it was me.' Her voice finally cracked. 'It was my fault – I was horrible to you.'

She turned and hugged him. Her face was soaking, all blotchy and red.

'I've…never…hit anyone…' she explained between sobs. 'In my whole life…I feel so ashamed…'

'It didn't hurt,' he said. 'Honestly. Ssh, it's OK.'

They kissed for a long time and held each other for longer. Then, as if it was the most natural thing in the world, Alex stood up, undressed and climbed into bed.

Ritch took off his clothes and got in beside her. Her skin felt warm and smooth.

She whispered, 'Do you have any condoms?'

He shook his head. 'I didn't think...'

Gently she moved her body against him. They kissed again and this time the kiss lasted until they both had to draw breath.

Afterwards she looked into his eyes and said, 'You must bring something with you next time, you silly boy.'

They hadn't gone all the way and yet when they did, weeks later, it felt just the same. Being close was what counted, truly. Since that first afternoon in her bed Ritch knew that Alex and he would always be one and the same.

The log-jam cleared down below. Some towing outfit had arrived and made a nice packet. The prices those swindlers charged, you'd feel less cheated if they held you up with a gun.

Ritch was still day-dreaming when the entryphone buzzed, then kept on buzzing. The cranky thing must have stuck. Eventually he found his walking stick and hopped inside to pick up.

'E-coli Pizzas,' he cracked. 'How may I help you?'

'Quit fooling around –'

The static was bad. Nothing came through for a while and then G's voice surfed in over the storm.

'– I just saw Ice dragging Alex into the underground car park. She was carrying a letter.'

'Stay there. I'll be down right away.'

Once Ritch got there G quit pacing the floor. More scared than angry, he moaned, 'You took your time. That sadist looks as high as a kite on some kind of dope.'

'The little creep's gonna retaliate first.'

Almost tripping over his stick Ritch hobbled across the kids' playground. If that rat hurt Alex...

'What are you – what are we gonna do when we get there?' wailed G.

'Leave that to me,' Ritch told him. 'Go ring the Law.'

'I was trying to, but all the pay-phone are out.'

'Shoot across to Mick's joint. They've got one fixed to the wall.'

'You come as well.'

'Just do it!'

G stopped in mid-stride, like a video on pause.

'Don't start anything until I get back.' He waited a while before racing off.

Slogging along Ritch thought, she won't understand. He had to go through with it anyhow: the final showdown with Ice. He had to, to save her. There was no other route.

He limped round to the car park and spied down the ramp. Only this entrance led into the derelict hole. Ice would see him coming from way too far off.

There was a utilities room by the top of the ramp. Every lock had been smashed. Ritch went in, opened the cable riser and then squeezed inside. The tunnel came out at the back of the cellar. With any luck he'd treat Ice to a real nasty surprise.

Ritch crawled into the dark, toting the walking stick hooked to his belt. The tunnel stank of rat's urine. He gagged the whole way. Each second counted but the bum leg slowed him up.

At the bottom he had to get down and slide along on his belly. Then the walls moved in tighter and the floor took a dip. As he slipped into a water-filled trough his mouth flooded with scum. Ritch couldn't breathe. He was five years old again, drowning. Thinking of Alex he splashed through to dry ground.

At last the tunnel came to an end. He craned his neck out and risked a squint round. Every lamp had been trashed. The place looked deserted, a winos' den full of used needles and broken booze bottles. Not one single motor. Who would be fool enough to park a set of wheels here?

In a corner close by, on a blanket, two silhouettes began struggling.

Alex yelled, 'No!'

Tumbling onto the concrete Ritch fell on the walking stick and snapped it in bits. The crack echoed loud the length of the cavern.

Ice hollered, 'Who's that? Who's there?'

Ritch's ambush was blown.

'It's me, you sick pervert.'

He staggered up to them out of the dark. Ice stopped hitting on Alex but kept the blade aimed at her throat.

'Let her go, now.' Ritch sounded reasonable. Then he said, 'Or I'll put a bullet right through your brain.'

Her clothes were mussed up and her long hair was in knots. The girl from the Village didn't react till the word bullet sank in.

'No, Ritchie.'

Alex screamed and tried to stand up. Ice pulled her back by the hair. From ten feet away Ritch could smell the glue streaming off him. His eyes looked like marbles rolling around in a skull. The lunatic junkie could barely see straight.

'Drop the knife,' Ritch threatened. 'Do it right now.'

He held his hands low, keeping the rod hidden. Tucked in the corner Alex glared at him, wildly mouthing, 'Don't do it. No.'

Ice knew that there were shooters galore all across the estate. Lots of guys owned one. You just had to figure out where to look and how much to pay...

The crazy thug flipped Ritch the finger. HATE was spelled out on the knuckles. A new bodged tattoo to match the one round his neck.

'You ain't gonna fire,' he slurred. 'You ain't really that hard.' He peered at Ritch through the gloom. 'I've seen you two lovers together. How d'you think your sweetheart would look with an extra-wide smile?'

The rat ran his tobacco-stained hand through Alex's hair, feinting the knife at her cheek as she shoved him away.

'Go ahead – cut her.' Ritch hefted the weapon. 'But if you do...say goodbye to this world.'

At that moment he meant every word.

Ice sucked his scabby knuckles. Drool ran down his chin. Was it true or a bluff? He was too stoned to tell.

Alex kicked and squirmed her way out of his reach. 'Don't harm him, Ritchie,' she begged. 'Anyone can see that he's ill. You promised to change. Now prove that you have.'

The way that she saw it, if anything happened, three lives would be wrecked.

'Yeah, you heard what she said,' Ice cackled. 'You're a new man.'

Leaning across the soiled blanket, the creep touched the front of Alex's sweater with his nicotined paw. She twisted around to hide her face in the corner. Ice laughed like a nut. He was losing the thread.

Ritch thought, am I meant to stand by while the rat does what he wants?

With Alex's back turned, he levelled the piece.

'Believe what you like. But I'm gonna start counting to three. And when I get to the end, if you ain't dropped that blade I start blasting away.'

'Your boyfriend ain't serious, is he?'

Ice looked at his hostage. She was staring at Ritch, violently shaking her head. He quickly covered the weapon.

'Sure I am. Try me.'

How long could he keep the glue-sniffer stalled?

Alex climbed to her knees, searching his eyes. She had to prevent this.

Ritch counted, 'One.'

As Ice put a hand on the wall Ritch took aim at his chest.

'Two.'

He thought, where the hell has G gone with that call to the cops?

The creep levered himself up off the floor. Alex began edging between them, inch by slow inch. Suddenly she spotted what Ice was too stoned to see.

'Three...'

Ice lurched to one side, looming above Alex, waving the kitchen knife over her head. Mouth twisted with rage, he tottered towards Ritch. Stopping three feet away, the rat raised his arm...then hurled the blade at the floor. It bounced high in the air.

Totally drained, Alex collapsed on the blanket. This was no lightning storm. No one as evil as Ice had ever touched her before.

The skinhead's knife lay on the concrete, tempting Ritch to stoop down, retrieve it and carve a trench in his face. Instead he stepped forward and hoofed it away.

'That ain't no gun,' Ice realised.

Good spot. Too bad – too late.

The rat threw a looping right hook. Ritch bobbed underneath, dropped the walking-stick stub and grabbed the thug by the waist. Wrestling to gain an advantage, the pair smashed to the ground.

Ice came up on top. Ritch was taller and heavier but the virus had weakened him. Ice clamped both hands round his prey's throat, tight as a car crusher's jaws.

Gasping for air, Ritch worked a knee between the thug's legs and drove home a jolt. That just made him meaner. The pit bull craned over and chewed his stitched ear.

Bright lights appeared on the ceiling where there'd been none before. But from where Ritch lay choking, the basement looked dimmer. Everything was fading, fading to grey.

'Leave him alone!'

Alex wrenched Ice away and pushed him flat on his back. Her eyes blazed. The girl was as strong as a bulldozer when she got mad.

At the top of the ramp a Law siren blared. Ice, the doped dummy, ran for the exit – right into the path of a patrol car that screeched down the slope. The cop riding shotgun leapt out and collared the skinhead. The driver switched on a torch and swept its beam round the hole.

Ritch rubbed his throat. 'You'll be safe enough now,' he croaked and kissed the top of Alex's head.

Wrapping herself in the blanket she tightened her

mouth. 'I was right. Arsonists do start fires to play with the flames.'

As the beam swept across her Ritch scuttled back up the riser. Feeling pleased to see the Law at a crime scene was a novel experience. But old habits die hard. They might bust his butt for the sake of old times.

When G dropped by to talk, later on in the week, and said, 'You're lucky to be here, you big bozo,' Ritch answered, 'It was only a virus.'

'You came close to death,' his pal said and passed him the red envelope. 'Wreaths are expensive.' They'd already had this argument once. He meant taking Ice on single-handed, not any cough.

Ritch slipped Alex's letter into his pocket. He had a real bad feeling about it.

'I'll be around for a while yet,' he promised. 'Relax, your money's safe.'

'All the guys in the neighbourhood send their regards. Kenny and Muff were gonna come over but something cropped up.'

The scholar disapproved.

'A Jag or a Merc?' Ritch asked.

'Something like that.'

'I bet it's a soft top. Muff's a sucker for those.'

Ritch had been out joy-riding enough times with the guy, he ought to know.

Down on the motorway a limo cut out of the rush hour and cruised down the hard shoulder. Some big-shot who thought he was too special to wait.

G prodded his glasses back on his nose and said, 'Ice is in jail, on remand till the trial. They've charged him with assault and abduction. The fool's gonna do time for sure,' probably hoping to give his convalescent buddy a boost.

The cops hadn't come calling on Ritch yet. Maybe, just like G, Alex wouldn't name names. Ritch had never felt less interested in that kind of talk though. The sun shone bright. The kid still shivered. He put his hand in his pocket and weighed the thick envelope.

'I couldn't care less,' he answered. 'I got bigger things on my mind than some psychotic screwball. From now on I'm all through with that stupid stuff.'

It was the first time he'd said so.

'Now you're talking.' G smiled a broad one.

'That's more like it. You know that makes sense.'

He reached in his jean jacket.

'Here, you big hero. This is from Lucy.'

It was a get-well card from his little sister. The crayon drawing on the front showed Ritch bandaged up tight, like a mummy. You could just see some teeth smiling through all the tape.

It was cute. 'Tell her thanks.'

G gave him another bag full of books. Ritch crowded them next to the chairs.

'If you don't make the grade as a lawyer you'll always be a shoo-in for postman.'

'My old man'll be real thrilled to hear it,' said G. 'The speed you read, I didn't think you'd be ready for more yet. But the artist insisted...'

'You ain't getting stuck on her, are you?' Ritch kidded the thin Romeo.

'You're worse than an old married man. You want everyone else to get spliced.' G patted his shoulder. 'No chance of that, pal. That girl and me are only good friends.'

They shot the breeze about this and that for a while,

and then Ritch's stomach let out a growl. The invalid offered to call in a plumber, but G insisted on frying his special omelette, which was two eggs lobbed in a pan with any scraps he could find.

Pots and pans crashed in the kitchen. Ritch opened the letter. Inside the envelope there were two sheets of notepaper smelling of the sandalwood oil Alex used on her hair:

> *Dear Ritch,*
>
> *I'm afraid this is going to be full of bad news. My parents have found out all about us (that disgusting boy, the car park and everything else). Things have been very hard for me here at home since. My mother is extremely unwell. The doctor seems to think she could be clinically depressed. She can't bear the idea of me going to court as a witness, getting all that publicity, and neither can I. Father wants us to move up to Edinburgh, where his parents live, but my mother won't go unless Gran agrees to come too.*

These past few days I've been feeling very down and confused. I know you saved me from something quite awful, yet a part of me feels that you enjoyed getting your own back. Perhaps if you'd had a real gun that horrid boy would be dead. However hard I try to forget it, the thought won't go away.

I really don't know what's going to happen. But until things settle down it's best that we don't see each other. I'll write again just as soon as I can.

All my love to you. Always.

Your Alex
XXXXX

He read the letter again, then a third time.

'What is it? Bad news?'

G balanced the plate of eggs and corned beef on Ritch's knee.

'No, good. It's good news. Thanks.'

Under the blanket he folded the pages.

'Is this my omelette?' Ritch forced a smile. 'Or

something you found living at the back of the stove?'

Poor Alex. He could imagine her parents piling on the agony. All that guilt. All that pressure.

Ritch hoped her old man burst a blood vessel. Her old lady as well. The wrong kind of boyfriend, a lousy kicking or two, and the maths teacher flipped.

Ritch thought, a marshmallow like that wouldn't last long in the schools around here.

G was telling him about college, his grant, the girl at the bookstore. Ritch wasn't listening. He thought, they think they know all about us? Don't make me puke.

The eggs tasted OK, but he'd lost his appetite. He ate half and then pushed the rest about on the plate. The evening traffic thinned to a trickle. G realised that the patient's mind was stuck someplace else, promised to drop by again later, said, 'Take it easy,' and split.

The hum of the lift died away. Ritch wondered how she was feeling, and how her parents had rumbled them. Had Alex caved in and confessed – out of exhaustion? Had she finally copped a bellyful of his old wild-ass ways?

Ritch had pulled off the rescue without anyone

getting hurt. He could have cut the creep up, instead he'd let it slide. Yet he was still getting the kiss-off. Deep down inside he knew that was so. It'd finally got to her. Ice snatching Alex had been the last straw.

Ritch closed his eyes and pictured her in her swim-suit, lying on the floor in his bedroom, chestnut hair spread out all round...

He grabbed his coat, scoured the flat for any loose change Gerry had missed, and then limped down to Mick's place.

The second the guy clocked Ritch's face he asked, 'What happened to you, Quasimodo?'

'I had a ruck with a bus,' claimed Ritch. 'Can I hop a ride to the Village?'

'Sure,' the cab boss nodded. 'I'll radio one in – if you got the fare.'

While they were waiting Mick said, 'You should have picked on one of my motors. They're a lot smaller.'

The joker didn't ask any more questions. His firm was third rate but the guy had real class.

*

At the end of her street Ritch paid off the driver with a fistful of silver and pennies. There wasn't enough for a tip, let alone the ride back.

The cabby counted it out. A few coppers over.

'Hey, thanks a lot. Now I can buy myself that little farm in the country.'

The rust-bucket kangarooed off coughing oil over all the flash cars.

When Ritch got to the house Alex was heading home with her cousin. He ran into them just as they were reaching the drive. Both girls gave him a look that could have turned lemons sourer. For once it was easy to see how they shared the same blood.

He said, 'Are you feeling OK?' There were dark rings under her eyes.

'Didn't you get my letter?' She looked deathly pale from staying awake half the night. 'We're moving to Scotland.'

'That's why I came.'

Clare linked arms against him. She had all the charm of a Holloway warder. 'No one invited you here,' she snarled. 'Why don't you leave us alone?'

Alex shushed her cousin, then said, 'It's all been too

much, Ritch. Everything's happening so fast. Honestly, truly, I need to...' She kneaded her temples. 'Perhaps I'll know my mind better after we've had a break.'

Man, did that make him queasy.

'But I had to whack him,' he pleaded. 'Payback didn't come into it. Can't you see?'

He meant not slicing Ice.

'Look, I don't want to debate this right now.' Or anything else. Emerald pools filled her eyes. 'Please, just go away.'

'Let me stay for a while.'

Clare passed her cousin a handkerchief, snorting, 'You heard – go away.' She'd hated him from the start.

'How about leaving us alone for a minute?' the sap heard himself begging.

He got hit with a real snotty laugh.

'She's my cousin, not my worst enemy.'

Alex wiped her eyes, tried to speak, but for once couldn't find the right words.

'You always were a foul influence,' accused Clare. 'Encouraging her to stop out and lie to her parents...'

Although Ritch hadn't wronged her, she was taking revenge.

'...I tried to tell her but she wouldn't listen. She fell head over heels.'

Jealousy. It's a poison. Clare was right about one thing though: he'd been no good for Alex. Just think of the horrors he'd hauled her through.

'Move out of our way.' She tried to drag Alex past.

Al had her cousin sussed, about half. Melodramatic. In the end not so harmless. It didn't take a genius to figure out where Clare's aunt and uncle had got the lowdown on Ritch.

'Were they pleased when you told them?' he asked her. 'Did it make everyone happy?'

'Don't be such a bully,' Alex found her tongue. 'She didn't mean to, it slipped out by accident.'

'Uh-huh. Right – under turbo assist.'

Jeez. She was defending the squealer. Ritch kicked the rear tyre on her old man's pig of a Volvo gleaming there in the drive. The car alarm treated the neighbours to an ear-splitting yowl.

Her dad shot out of the house. With reflexes that sharp, the old geezer was probably head of their local watch scheme. He zapped the alarm and scrunched down the drive yelling, 'Get away from my daughter.'

Alex tugged Ritch's sleeve. 'If you leave now, I promise to write.'

He shook his head and planted both feet in the gravel, bent on persuading her. He reached for her hand, she pulled it away.

The old fella saw the manoeuvre and started to trot. His face was mottled with anger when he puffed into range. Throwing an arm round his daughter and niece he demanded, 'Haven't you caused enough trouble?' not caring for once about any public display.

Ritch showed him the unmarked side of his mug. 'I love her,' he said. 'She loves me too.'

The accountant made a quick assessment of the slum kid, took in the bruises, the torn jeans, then sneered like a fool.

'How dare you!' Spittle sprayed in the air. 'My daughter's not one of your drug addict friends.' For a jumped-up bookkeeper he owned plenty of nerve.

'You'll never split us up.' Ritch reached out once more. 'We'll stay together whatever you do.'

Alex looked from her father, to Ritch, then back again.

The accountant shuffled in front of the girls and knocked the outstretched hand flat.

'Get off my property,' the old geezer bellowed. 'If you pester us again I'll see you in jail.'

He went to grab Ritch by the scruff of the neck, hoping to frog-march him out of their lives. The kid from the estate flinched and threw up a guard. Ice's vicious gang beating still played on his mind.

Alex shouted, 'Watch out, Dad.'

Her father dodged aside and slipped on the gravel. Crashing face down, he hit his head on a rock at the edge of the drive. A trickle of blood ran down one cheek. Alex stared at her father, sprawling dazed in the dust, then she turned to Ritch holding his fist in the air.

'It's all over now,' she said. Her eyes looked dead as a shark's. 'You've had your last chance.'

And he knew that was it.

Three strikes and you're out.

Ritch hung around till her old man sat up and refused

Clare's offer to phone the police. With Al mopping his blood into her hankie the accountant said, 'This was all my own fault. I'll be fine, let him go.'

Why not? After all, he'd won. Again.

As Ritch limped down the road he thought, I'll never forget her.

If only he could rewind back to the Mission that night.

A roughneck like him, someone classy like Alex: it could have panned out. He wouldn't have made her feel stupid or fouled up her career – not now, he wouldn't. Living happily ever after, was that such a big thing to ask?

He stopped to rest at the corner. She was helping her old man stumble back to their house, her temporary prison until they moved north. He thought, being non-violent ain't so simple, whatever she says.

Maybe if he stuck around G for a few more years he'd get it right. Maybe he'd be a vet too, some day, like Alex wanted. Ritch sucked his teeth, and started back home.

Later, hanging on the off-licence bell, he thought, a year's a long time, people change. This ain't over yet. They might be moving to Scotland but their daughter would still go to Cambridge. That was forty miles, just a train journey away.

He'd give his all to win Alex over. No one was claiming that it was going to be easy though.

Nothing ever is when love walks out your door.

Other Black Apples
to get your teeth into...

WEIRDO'S WAR

Michael Coleman

Daniel is known as Weirdo because he enjoys doing things at school that others think strange: working out mathematical calculations and formulas for everything, doing his homework and being on his own. Tosh couldn't be more different: hanging around with his 'friends' who use him as a butt of their jokes and picking on others, such as Daniel. So when they find themselves sharing lodgings on an Outward Bound weekend neither is too happy. And things can only get worse when they're involved in a terrible accident and become trapped underground together…

'Tense and psychological.'
The Times

Shortlisted for the Carnegie Medal

1 86039 812 X   £3.99

JUST SIXTEEN

Jean Ure

Priya was special and I wanted to be special for her.

Sam and his friends enjoy boasting about their successes with girls. But then Sam meets Priya and finds himself getting to know a girl who he can really talk to, who he doesn't see as just a sex object or trophy. Of course he fancies her too, and Priya feels the same way. Making love feels right for both of them, but then Priya discovers she's pregnant… Will their unborn baby bind them together or tear them apart?

1 84121 453 1   £4.99

HOROWITZ HORROR

Anthony Horowitz

A spine-tinglingly scary collection of chilling tales from top thriller writer Anthony Horowitz.

Some mysterious deaths linked to a second-hand camera; a boy trapped inside a computer game; a frightening journey on a bus that doesn't seem to exist, and a terrifying dream that comes true...these are just some of the stories in this new collection of nine nasty horror stories.

Brilliantly written, atmospheric and gripping, Horowitz Horror will appeal to all lovers of the macabre and the mysterious.

'Move over Roald Dahl, here comes Anthony Horowitz'
Young Telegraph

1 84121 455 8   £4.99

LITTLE SOLDIER

Bernard Ashley

Kaninda is an orphan from the war in Lasai, East Africa, who ends up in a London comprehensive school – having been a real soldier in the rebel Kibu army, carrying weapons and using them. But clan and tribal conflicts are everywhere, and on the south London streets it's estate versus estate.

Kaninda just wants to get back to his own war and to take revenge on his enemies, but along with Laura Rose, the daughter of his new adopted family, he is slowly drawn into a local war caused by the hit-and-run injury of a child from one of the estates.

An emotionally powerful, hard-hitting story, with scenes from the African civil war as well as current inner-city conflict.

'Bernard Ashley at his most brilliant.'
Chris Powling

1 86039 879 0   £4.99